Love Among the Cannibals

Books by Wright Morris in Bison Book Editions

Date of first publication at the left

Also available from the University of Nebraska Press

Conversations with Wright Morris (BB 630)
Edited with an introduction by Robert E. Knoll

Wright Morris

LOVE AMONG THE CANNIBALS

University of Nebraska Press • Lincoln and London

First Bison Book printing: 1977

Most recent printing indicated by first digit below:
2   3   4   5   6   7   8   9   10

Library of Congress Cataloging in Publication Data
Morris, Wright, 1910–
  Love among the cannibals.
  Reprint of the 1st ed. published by Harcourt, Brace,
New York.
    I. Title.
[PZ3.M8346Lo5] [PS3525.O7475]   813'.5'2   76–16574
ISBN 0–8032–0880–4
ISBN 0–8032–5842–9 pbk.

Reprinted by arrangement with the author.

Manufactured in the United States of America.

"Nay further, we are what we all abhor, *Anthropophagi* and Cannibals, devourers not onely of men, but of our selves; and that not in an allegory, but a positive truth. . . ."

SIR THOMAS BROWNE, Religio Medici

The *manners*, the manners: where and what are they, and what have they to tell?

HENRY JAMES, The American Scene

Book One

This chick, with her sun-tan oil, her beach towel, her rubber volleyball, and her radio, came along the beach at the edge of the water where the sand was firm. Soft sand shortens the legs and reduces their charms, as you may know. This one pitched her camp where the sand was dry, slipped on one of these caps with the simulated hair, smoked her cigarette, then went in for a dip. Nothing particular, just a run-of-the-mill sort of chick. She was out beyond the surf when I noticed that the tide was dampening her towel. I got up and dragged it back alongside our own. When she came out of the water I explained what had happened and she thanked me without being coy. She dried her hair and accepted one of our cigarettes. We got to talking, the way you do, and since everyone in California is from somewhere else it gives you something, at the start, to talk about. She was

9

from Dubuque. The one in Iowa. Married a boy from Port Chester during the war. That didn't pan out, so she had come to California on a scholarship good for fifty bucks. All she had to do was earn her own living and raise the other three hundred twenty-five. She lived with two other chicks at the school and they all worked as waitresses at the same Wilshire drive-in. They all liked California, but they thought the people were cold. Her childhood had not been too happy and her mother often complained that her father was too small for a satisfactory sexual partner. Her mother didn't use those words, of course, but that was what she meant. If her father had not been so *conventional* it might have worked out. Why were men so perverse they always had to be on *top*?

That's what she said. She said why are men so perverse. Then she asked me if I had any ideas, and I had a few ideas but what I said was that the *conventional* sort of thing, with maybe a million years behind it, had a lot to recommend it. How do you know what's conventional *now*, she said, was conventional *then*? Her shift at the drive-in began before I had an answer to that.

I'd never seen her before. I'll probably never see her again. She was twenty-two or -three, I suppose, and I'll be forty-one the ninth of September, having lived and loved more or less conventionally. Things can change in twenty years. More, I mean, than I have changed myself. When I was her age I didn't know beans. She knows too much.

I did ask her, just before she left, what she thought of that movie of the Kansas picnic where the frustrated schoolteacher tears the shirt off the visiting bum. I was born in Kansas. I went to a lot of picnics as a boy. But in my time, the big scene would have been the other way around. The lady's, not the gent's, shirt would have to be torn. I asked her what she thought of that scene and she said it was a fine job, artistically speaking. You see what I mean? Things have changed. I carried her volleyball and wet towel to the road, where she took a bus, one that went down Wilshire, then I bought two cans of beer for Mac and myself and walked back to the beach.

I

My story begins, like everything else, on the beach. Beaches are the same the world over, you peel down, then you peel off; they serve you up raw meat, dark meat, or flesh nicely basted in olive oil. A strip of sun and sand where the sex is alert, the mind is numb. The beach in question, one of the best, is near where Sunset Boulevard meets the sea. I don't mean to be ironic. California is that way naturally. It's hard to do malice to California, but this particular strip might have been in Acapulco, or down in Rio, or along the Riviera. If it's world brotherhood you want, go to the beach. If you like parallels, the beach is where we came in, and where we'll go out. Having crawled from the sea, we're now crawling back into it. That solution of salt in the blood is calling us home. And in a mammary age, what better place to compensate for an unsuckled childhood? Where

13

else, these days, does the pretty matron shyly lower her bra straps, hugging her charms? Not to nourish the future, alas, but to preserve, in sun oil, the present. A season in the sun before going under. Is that what we want? My friend Mac has a colleague who wears on her tanned thigh the white shadow of a man's hand—his own, as it happens. A climax, of course, to her night-club act. A purely professional assist, in every respect. They often pass the time at the beach together, and one man's hand is as good as another's. She sings his songs, so he really belongs in the act.

When people ask me where I ran into Mac, I say the war. We have the stamp of things that came out of it. I've pieced together that Mac was born in Brooklyn, but I've never really heard him say so. He doesn't talk. I mean he doesn't articulate. If he's in a friendly, expressive mood he might sing his own songs, one of Cole Porter's, or variations on a number called *Dancing in the Dark*. That's Mac. If you add Noel Coward you've covered the field. If he has ever felt anything else I don't think he would recognize it. Which leaves me with a real problem. How to keep him up-to-date. I take an old cliché, soak him in it, then give it just that squeeze of the lemon that leads him to think he thought of it himself. In the flush of that sort of emotion he can speak.

"Man," he will bark, "it's great!"

In the song-and-dance business self-confidence helps.

Mac is thirty-eight, just three years my junior, but he looks a good deal younger. He has a round, bland, background-music sort of face. He tends to run a little heavy, his complexion is mottled with what I suppose was teenage smallpox, and he gives strangers the impression he's a little deaf. He isn't, but he seldom hears anything. When I'm in a rare sympathetic mood I tell the chicks that he's listening to his own music. But he's not. Nor is it what you would call a blank. The absence of any popular song to describe the vacant moods Mac passes his life in will leave most of his life a mystery. Two or three times a month he will roll over and say—he never thinks of anything unless he's lying down—"I ever tell you how I shot down that ME-109?"

In fifteen years you can shoot down a lot of 109's. But that event keeps coming back to him like the theme of one of his songs—a hit song, I suppose, he is still trying to find the music for. He looks to me for the words, but I don't have them. I never shot down an ME-109 myself.

15

I had lived with Irwin K. Macgregor for eight months in England without speaking to him. But that was not unusual. Nobody did. He was not the silent type, but the army had silenced him. Like a lot of silent men, he didn't have much to say, but in an inarticulate sort of way he can be fluent. This fluency consists of a theme and variation. The theme is, "Man, it's great!" The variation, "It's great, man!" If you know the army, you know what it would do to a vocabulary like that. "It's great, man!" will cover most of the verbal problems in the song business, but the army was no song, so Mac had nothing to say. Nothing at all, I mean, until he met me.

Mac was no great shakes as a pilot but we both fagged out the same cold winter, and we were sent upcountry to the same warm spa to recuperate. That's where we met. The place featured the usual lousy food, but some nice girls from Holland and a grand piano. I didn't know till he gave the stool a spin, and sat on it, that he played. I'd sit down at one end of the room, with a book, and watch this army-silenced guy dust off the stool with his knuckles, then squat on it and *talk*. A fluent keyboard lover. A real poet, of sorts, on the black keys. One day he played with a little more schmaltz than usual, and although we hadn't exchanged a word he looked up and said:

"Like that, eh?"

"It's not a bad tune," I said, since it sounded familiar.

"It's great, man!" he said. "I wrote it."

And he had. I could name you, but I won't, about a half-dozen tunes he had written before I met him. Not bad, not good. Lacking the master touch. The sort of *unheard* music you need to fill out a TV program. But his piano was good. It was the piano that gave him his start. He could have sat out the war in a Fort Dix jazz band but he got this idea that he wanted to fly. He thought the war had come along so he could pick up, without charge, the rudiments. He did, all right, and as he points out himself—that's where he met me. I couldn't do much for his talent, but I could give the lyrics a certain touch. If the lyrics were *good*—I mean if the clichés were coined before he was—he had the sort of talent that could almost live up to them. What I'm saying is, as he puts it, we make a great team.

There have been so many corny movies about jazz pianists I don't have to tell you about them. That's how he was. I mean he was like *all* of them. He believed. He even believed in his own stuff. After he met me there was some point in it—some point, that is, believing in *my* stuff—but up until then it was all a matter of faith. Until he met me all of his songs were songs without words.

17

I took his music and pasted the right sort of labels on it. I used to do that sort of thing for nothing, what we referred to in my youth as amusement, and I found it more amusing than trying to read a book. Sitting there, day after day, I heard the same tunes over and over, and I found it entertaining to write a set of lyrics for some of them. One little tune I liked went something like this:

> Roses are nice, violets are too,
> But tulips are what I share with you.
> Stamen, pistil and pollen connect,
> The tulips of Kansas with old Utrecht.

I had reference to a particular piece of light meat from Utrecht. One day Mac played this tune and from my corner of the room I chipped in with the lyrics. It made quite an effect.

"Man, it's great!" he barked, and with that modest statement the song team of Macgregor and Horter was born. It didn't help me with the maid from Holland, but it settled me with Macgregor. "You got a talent, man!" he said. "You know what I mean?" As it happened, I did. We've been inseparable, as our billing says, ever since.

It's probably fair to say, as Mac often does, that

I've made him whatever he is—*is* being a man with a fat check from ASCAP every month. In the trade we are sometimes referred to as the poor man's Rodgers & Hart, since the big-time money has a way of eluding us. It might be that my lyrics, like some cough drops, dissolve very pleasantly on the tongue but have a way of coming back, like the taste of onions, during the night. I don't really know. But something like the taste of onions is at the back of my mouth right now.

In the *Who's Who in the Missouri Valley*—in it at one time, that is—you will see my picture and find me listed as the Shelley of the corn belt. The next year I was drafted. That makes me sixteen years a poet *manqué*. I understand that the war made some poets the way a man is said to make a woman, but that wasn't my war, and it had another effect on me. The only poetry I now hear is when Mac brings a chick to the apartment and plays my recording of Eliot reading *The Waste Land*. He has the record nicked so it retracks when the voice says:

"Hurry up, please, it's time!"

Something about Eliot's Oxford accent seems to do the trick. It's never long before he gets up and turns the record off, and the lights on. Although I've stopped writing it myself, I'm responsible for spreading some pretty good lines. Trapped with a chick of the brainy type Mac will say:

> "Does the imagination dwell the most
> Upon a woman won or a woman lost?"

If she says lost, he dates her. If she doesn't, he claims he hasn't missed anything.

Before you feel sorry for either of us, let me tell you that we spend our time on the beach, where, if you had our time and money, you'd like to spend yours. We came here, instead of Bermuda, where the sun is also shining, because I had, and sold, this idea for a new musical. New? Well, something in the line of a Latin-American *Porgy and Bess*. Yankee money, Latin passion, good-neighbor policy, everything. I've been to Mexico, which takes care of *that*, and Mac has listened to a lot of Xavier Cugat. We don't want it so Latin it might alienate Uncle Sam. Three of the major studios fought for it, and we are now living in what they call a château, in one of the fire-trap canyons, with a view of all the water that is out of reach in case of fire. Mac has a piano, and I have all day at the beach. What I do, I can do anywhere, but

Mac can only sound chords at night, or very early morning on the St. Regis roof. He sleeps under the beach umbrella most of the day, then we go out to eat where they have background music, with a girl in the foreground singing Macgregor & Horter's latest hit. A little after midnight we drive back up the canyon and go to work. Something Mac once read in a muscle magazine led him to feel that sex drains a man's creative energy. He means the same night. It doesn't seriously handicap a song writer. Sex is something he takes like vitamins, and it has nothing to do with immortal love, tenderness, loss of sleep, and songs like *Stardust*. As Mac says himself:

"Sex is sex. You know what I mean?"

I do. It is part of my job. The problem is to find a nice respectable chick who needs a little push along, professionally, and who doesn't mind a little do-re-mi from a respectable guy. They're not too hard to find. A little French Bikini number, who needed a very long push, had been on Mac's hands for the past three weeks, but she had this idea that you don't need a voice in the song racket. You don't. But you need more than one close friend.

That side of my colleague's nature is cut and dried, offers little in the way of complications, and leaves him fairly famished for what he calls the *real thing*. The real thing is hard to define, but roughly it's what Charlie Chaplin found, beginning with Paulette Goddard. We might call it *The Million-Dollar Baby in the Five-&-Ten Weltanschauung*. I think he got it from the song, which he ran into a little early, but he was, and is, precocious about songs. As another man stumbles on *Jean Christophe*, Kahlil Gibran, or Dale Carnegie, Mac stumbled on the Million-Dollar Baby in the five-and-ten. That did it. That's what he means by *heart*.

"It's got no heart, man!" he'll say, so I'll take whatever it is and slip in a few words about how he found her in the automat. A girl with a green stain on her finger from a piece of Christmas jewelry can name her price. Mac will double it.

Like a talent scout in Woolworth's basement, Mac likes to hang around the record department, waiting for some Million-Dollar Baby to buy one of his songs. When she does he will lean over and say, "Like that, eh?" As a rule she does, having bought it. He will then introduce himself as the author, and the next thing you know he asks the chick if she can sing. Did you ever hear of a girl in a dime store who couldn't sing? I suppose we have roughly half a million records proving that not one of

them can, but the way some of them *can't* is interesting.
Mac has turned up a dozen or so of them. Any one of
these girls will tell you that Mac has a heart of gold,
combined with the loftiest Father's Day sentiments. All
of which is true. His Million-Dollar Babies are left un-
touched. They are all heart, having nothing in common
with the chicks, of a respectable sort, who need a little
practical push along. They can be found in dime stores,
drugstores, hot-dog stands, orange-drink shops, and all
those places Charlie Chaplin had the knack of turning
them up. Nowadays they can also be flushed at the beach.
Million-Dollar Babies with that spring-green Christmas
jewelry look.

You never know the other side of an army man until
you see him in mufti. But Mac has no mufti. He stepped
out of one uniform into what I'll have to call another.
If you have sometimes wondered who it is who really
wears the two-tone ensembles that set the new car styling,
Mac is your man. That's why I keep him down at the
beach. He's quite a sight on the beach as well, in his
Hawaiian shorts, made of coconut fiber, a cerise jacket
with a bunny-fur texture, a sea-green beret, and something like an ascot looped at his throat. Those shops that
have the latest thing for men always have something,

hidden in one of the drawers, too early for anybody else but just right for Mac. On the beach I let him wear it. He still looks better with it on than off. He has one of those complexions that will never tan, so he passes the day under the beach umbrella. Having no complexion problems I lie in the sun and watch the chicks go in and out of the water. When the beach is crowded I listen for the up-and-coming clichés. That particular morning it wasn't crowded; we had a little morning fog, which is customary, but I rather like the beach in a cloud of fog. There you are; the sound of the sea is off behind the wall.

This little chick with her hair in a pony tail came up from behind us, sprinkled a little sand on me, then pitched her camp where the tide had smoothed the sand. She spread out her little towel, let down her straps, put on her gem-studded glasses with the built-in visor, daubed Noxzema on her nose, then lit up a Parliament and smoked. I thought the little leather case might have her lunch, her radio, and her sun-tan lotion, but this was no run-of-the-mill sort of chick. Not on your life. She opened it, cranked it, and put a record on the gramophone. Owing to the radio Mac was playing, we didn't hear her taste in music till he turned it off. A sultry-type songbird was crooning a number entitled "What Next?" That happened to be the last song we had written with a chance to catch on. The songbird was the not-so-little girl we call Pussy, the one with Mac's hand on her thigh, who specializes in what I call Music for Leching, without accompaniment. She sings under the name of Faith Amor. The one exception to my practice of using clichés, and not writing them, will be found in "What Next?" I had to write them. It explains the song's brand-new old look.

> What next?
> The life of love I knew
> No longer loves
> The things I do.
> What next?

When Mac heard those moving lines he sat up and barked, "Man, it's great! You know what I mean?"

This little chick really did.

"Ah think she is simply *wonnaful*," she said, modestly pulling up one suit strap. "If Miss Ah-moh does it, I just have to have it. Ah reahly do."

If you keep your ear to the ground for clichés, as I have to, you get these shockers. First you hear it, then you meet it in the flesh. Since Mac gives the impression of being a little deaf, she turned her blinkers on me.

"It's a nice song," I said. "What's the girl's name?"

Nothing rocks these chicks back so much as to hear they are mad about someone you never even heard of. She rocked back and said, "You nevah hurt of Miss Ah-moh?"

"You mean Pussy?" I said. "The chick on the strip?"

That cut her. You could see where she was cut.

"Pussy can do a nice piece, all right," I said, "if she's got the right material."

"Ah'm sho yoh can't mean Miss Ah-moh," she replied. "Ah nevah hurt Miss Ah-moh refurt to as Pussy."

"Her mummy calls her Pussy, her daddy calls her Pussy, her friends call her Pussy, and we call her Pussy."

"Yoh ackshilly know huh?"

"Mr. Macgregor here does," I said, giving Mac the nod. "He wrote the song foh huh." I have to watch myself with these Suthun belles, since I tend to imitate their lingo.

"Yoh ackshilly dit?" she said, looking at Mac. Mac ackshilly did, but I could sympathize with her. "Ah feel chus mortafite, Mistuh MacGraw—" she began, but if you're going to follow what it is she says I ought to stop telling you how she sounds. But if what she said really mattered, I'd translate it for you. It's all in how she sounds. What she went on to say was that if she had half the sense she was born with, a doubtful statement, she would have known it was the song, not just the ah-tist, that appealed to her. She managed to say that, then she looked at Mac as if talking to him would move him to speech.

"Pussy hams it up a little," I put in, "but it's not a bad piece."

She wiggled like a wet puppy on her towel, then she pinched herself and asked Mac if she was asleep or if she was awake. That was actually one that Mac might have answered, but he let it pass. Then she wanted to know if we thought she was crazy, a young unchaperoned little girl like herself, coming down to the beach with nothing but her record player and her Parliaments. I was about to answer that one when she sighed, then said:

"Mistuh MacGraw, ah get so sick an' tahd talkin' to mahself."

Mac generally looks so dead that any sign of life in him makes quite an impression. It made one on her. It made one on both of us. He suddenly sat up, leaning forward so far that the crucifix he wears around his neck swung free on its chain, showing the 18-carat stamp. He's not religious, but he believes in playing the odds. I could see the idea drip through his mind that there was a song here, a *great* one, and the words "so sick an' tired talkin' to myself" formed on his lips. Then it crossed his mind why he thought so. Someone had already done it. The wind of hope that had filled him seemed to leak out through his pores.

"Yoh know why ah come to the beach, Mistuh Mac-Graw? Ah come to thaw out. Ah was nevah so colt any-wheah in mah life as ah am out heah."

She shivered. If I had half the brains I was born with, I would have heard the alarm right there. Mac's alarm, I mean. The buzzer that rings when one of his Million-Dollar Babies turns up.

"It's a nasty climate—" I said, edging away. "You freeze in the fog, then—"

"Honey—" she said, giving herself a little hug, "ah doan mean that climate. Ah mean the hu-man climate. Ah nevah crossed paths with so many colt shoulters in all mah life."

In a moment of excitement he can hardly bear, Mac will take off whatever hat he is wearing, run one hand through his hair, then put the hat back on, pulled down tight. He did that. Then he looked at me and said, "Crossed paths, man! Crossed paths an' cold shoulders!"

His eyes were on me, but they were actually leafing through our song-title file. If "Crossed Paths" wasn't there now, it soon would be.

"Miss—" I began, but she was telling Mac that the only friend she had was her little record player, and by that she meant it was the only friend she had of the masculine sex. Was she out of her mind to think her little gramophone was her boy friend? Well, she did. It just went to prove how lonely she was. She was one of these chicks who close or flutter their eyelids whenever their mouth is open, acting on the same principle as these dolls with the weights in their heads. I couldn't get a word in edgewise. Her pretty little cold shoulders were covered with duck bumps. I thought Mac would take his shirt off and wrap it around her, but he was too excited, too full of the *big* one, so all he did was jam the hat down around his ears, then say:

"Baby—you sing?"

"Mistuh MacGraw!" she said, shocked with recognition. "Why, *Mis*tuh MacGraw."

"Miss—" I began.

"What in the wohld should evah make you think so,

29

Mistuh MacGraw? Ah do sing. Ah suppose ah should say ah wanna sing."

"Miss Garland—" I said. That clicked. I mean that cut her to the quick.

"Harcum," she said. "Miss Billie Harcum. Ah'm a stootun of Marlene Mazda Joyce, although yoh-all probly know huh, an' refuh to huh as somethin' else."

"Muzzy Joyce has some nice contacts, Miss Harcum," I said. "We sometimes find a cage for her little songbirds. You dance?"

"Why, Mistuh—"

"Horter. Of Macgregor & Horter."

"Ah'm the awfullust fool, Mistuh Hortuh. Ah know yoh name as well as mah own."

"Let's focus on Mac here then," I said. "The name is Mac*gregor*, not MacGraw, but he'll probably insist that you call him Mac."

"Oh, Mistuh Macgregaw!"

"My name is Earl," I went on, "but I don't insist on it."

"Uhl? Ah chus love Uhl as a name."

"We're not casting right now, Miss Harcum, but we have a small spot for some dark-complected dancers— Mexicali roses instead of Memphis roses, if you know what I mean."

She did. I waited to see if she could take it, and she took it.

"You'll need a little more color," I said, sizing her up. "The shade we're going to want is octoroon, or light mulatto—"

When I said mulatto she darkened to the shade I had in mind. Over the years I've noticed that a flush of indignation does more for a girl than Max Factor. There's more to flush in a woman, that is, than her face and eyes.

"You'll do if you can dance, honey," I said, and she suddenly saw right through me. I was a *card*. It had taken her all that time to catch on. I didn't really mean what I'd said about mulatto, it was just my way of pulling her pretty leg. She put it out where I could reach it, and said:

"Mistuh Hortuh, ah'm essenchuly a singah. A singah of the contnental type."

Continental-type singers, *aus* Weehawken and Memphis, are almost as rare as girls who sing in dime stores.

"What we *need* is dancers, Miss Harcum," I began, but Mac sat up suddenly and barked:

"Baby, can you take it?"

"Take it?" echoed Miss Harcum. Fearing the worst, she turned to me.

"We have a little test number, Miss Harcum," I said.

31

"If a girl can't take it—" I rolled my eyes, shrugged my shoulders.

"Can ah try—right heah, Mistuh Hortuh?"

"Sure, baby!" barked Mac. "If you'll turn that thing off—" and he wagged his hand at her whining record player. I don't sing our stuff often, but when I do Mac knows I like it quiet. Our little cannibelle number, as a matter of fact, is a litmus test. The chick can take it or leave it, and we can take or leave the chick. Miss Harcum wiggled over to switch off her machine, then she came over like a seal with a fish at its nose, and let me have the benefit of her pretty little duckies. I wet my lips, huskily crooned:

> "Baby cannibelle, once you try it,
> I'm the dark meat in your diet,
> You eat me while I eat you,
> Since it's the economical thing to do,
> Baby, baby can-ni-bellllle!"

Well, they don't do it so much any more, but she almost swooned. The Memphis type, *her* type, don't go in for playing it cool. She bit down on her lip, gasped for air, scooped little holes in the sand to hide her feet in, and gave no thought to the fact that both of her straps were down.

32

"Man," bellowed Mac, "she can take it! You know what I mean? She took it!"

"Oh, Mistuh Mac—"

"—gregor," I said. "The number's not particularly Latin-American, but it is *muy* Acapulco," giving the *muy* a roll that made it clear just what I meant.

"Aca-pulco?" she said. "Now did you evah— Ah'm invited to a pahty of some folks who just come from Acapulco. Theatuh people. You would know theah names. Ah'm invited but ah jus got too much self-respeck, I suppose."

"What kinda party is it, baby?" said Mac, since he loved nonrespectable parties.

"It's not the kinda pahty a respectable gurl is seen at alone."

I got the picture pretty well, and said, "Too bad all our nights are sewed up, Miss Harcum, but since Mac, here—"

"Baby—" said Mac, "when is it?"

"This particulah pahty just so happens to be tonight, Mistuh MacGraw."

"Baby—" chanted Mac, but in his excitement he forgot what he meant to say. But I hadn't. When a chick has passed the Horter test, it's always the same.

"You happen to have a girl friend, Miss Harcum?" I said.

"Mistuh Hortuh—" she said, fluttered her eyes as if the idea of a girl friend left her nonplused. It gave me time to slip a pencil out of Mac's shirt pocket, tear off a piece of his score. When her eyes stopped fluttering it crossed her mind that she did have a girl friend, one she worked with, and being theatuh people they all more or less lived in the same house. I took the address, the telephone number, and to make sure we would find the place after dark we drove her home and dropped her off on our way to eat.

This car the studio put at our disposal was in the quiet, unassuming good taste of a hot-rod parts manufacturer on his day off. Fireman red, with green leather upholstery, it had a crush-proof steering wheel, a crush-proof dash, compartments in the doors for whisky and soda, and a record player where the glove compartment usually is. We didn't even have to buy our own records. They supplied us with them.

I'd say one of Mac's ideas of heaven is to have Eddie Duchin playing Cole Porter while we cruise along the coast highway toward Santa Barbara. You don't have to whistle at the girls in this car, just sit in it with the top down, the music going, while you drive along the strip. This little chick and her friends lived in Westwood, in one of those attractive slums for tomorrow, a cool arrangement of glass and tin sloped to catch the heat. This chick had sworn her girl friends would be dying to meet me, an actual living man who wrote song lyrics, but she came down the steps alone, and joined us in the front. I must say she looked sharp. You know how these little girls learn to walk so they make a sharp clack on the pavement, and almost whinny when they pull up alongside your fence.

She climbed in—she got in between us—then she said she just *had* to be frank with me, and that her girl friends didn't feel they should be running around with a man my age. "Well, what age am I?" I said, since I hadn't mentioned my age. "All ah said was you certainly weren't over forty," she replied. I could see she pulled that deal just to flatter Mac, in his baby-face thirties, and at the same time have the two of us to herself. All the time she put on this little act her hand was on my knee, not Mac's, indicating that a man my age offered certain advantages.

Anyhow, I went to this party without a chick. We drove back to Sunset, I remember, into that section they call Bel Air, then we drove into the hills where the movie stars live. You can't bring the Riviera over in crates, the way Citizen Kane would have liked to, but you can name the streets Cannes, Antibes, Monaco, with an Italian wing running from Amalfi to Sorrento. We took the French wing, that night, and followed it to the summit of the hill, where we curved along the vine-covered wall of a château. So that the effect wouldn't be lost, or if you came up at night and might have missed it, the drive in went across a drawbridge over a moat. Inside the open court, about the size of a gym, there were representative sports cars of all nations, with a patriotic sprinkling of Thunderbirds. On the East Coast that would mean money, but here on the West Coast a soda jerk, willing to choose between a chick and a Thunder-bird, can have the Thunderbird. He lives in a closet, gulps his sandwich at the counter, and can't afford the salve for his athlete's foot, but when you see him on Sunset he's on a par with the movie stars. Unless they get off the highways, it leaves most movie stars with no place to turn.

Surrounded with all that quiet, imported good taste, our bright fire wagon had a certain class, and I left it where we could sneak off early, since I intended to.

One of these professional catering outfits had taken over the place. They had a fellow in the yard to lead you to the right door, a man at the door to size you up and frisk you, then one in the hall to guide you to the proper facilities. One of the minor dividends of forty-one years, fifteen of them passed among the gay counterfeiters, is that you can size up a piece of scenery pretty fast. The way these caterers knew their way around they probably lived in it. This mansion full of trophies—they had a viking sled with the reindeer harnessed in the main hallway—was probably rented out, furnished, for parties of this type. This one had been given an Acapulco flavor by stringing a fish net along the stairway, and scenting the place with the smell of Mexican cigarettes. They had a Mariachi outfit from Olvera Street, featuring an old man, his shoulders snowy with dandruff, who would let out that *yip* so characteristic of carefree, child-like, passionate Mexican life. The drinks were served in those blurred Mexican glasses, by waiters in creaky huaraches, and *aficionados* were encouraged to take their tequila straight. I'm nothing if not an *aficionado,* and I attracted more than the usual attention by scoffing at the plate of sliced limes, and crying for salt. I had spent most of one summer mastering tequila and salt. You sprinkle a little salt on the back of your hand, where you can lick it off, like a tourist, or by tapping the wrist, sharply, get the salt to hop into your mouth. I did, then raised my eyes to see—the way a man meets his fate in the movies—a woman, a young woman, who had just entered the room. The directness of her gaze caught me unprepared. I returned it, that is. The word chick—the word I *rely* on—did not come to mind. This tremendous girl—the scale of this girl made me step back a pace to see her—wore one of the flowers, one of the favors for the ladies, in her hair. That's all I could tell you. I turned away at that point to collect myself. It took me more than a moment. The jigger-size glass that held my tequila was slippery on the outside from what I had spilled. You know the feeling you have that in your grasp, *within* your grasp, you have the dream that has always escaped you—followed by the feeling that your eyes, and your heart, have cheated you again. When I turned she was gone. Gone. Had she really been there? I walked back to the main hall where I could see up the curve of the stairs, where the women congregated; pretty good-looking women, in the main, thanks to the California sun. But this girl was not there. Looking up the flight of stairs it occurred to me that I wouldn't know this girl by how she looked—I didn't *know* how she looked—I would only recognize her by how I felt. How did I feel? The way I often feel in elevators.

They had a table of food in the center of the hall, one of these smorgasbord setups where you help yourself, and just to occupy myself I selected a plate of food. I have to do that for Mac, anyhow, otherwise he will eat nothing but stuffed olives, *stuffed* olives being for him what *baba au rhum* is for me. A symbol of the carefree, indulgent life lived by the rich in the Great Bad Places. I let him have some pumpernickel to settle his liquor, then I found him very chummy with the Señorita, a bugle-voiced Mariachi singer from First Avenue and 96th. Since Miss Harcum had brought him to this party, I brought him back to the main hall, where she was waiting, having sprayed herself with something irresistible. I got myself some stuffed celery hearts and a tall drink with the cidery flavor of Sidral, then stepped into a room off the main hall that was not occupied. It had some comfortable chairs, and a big window that looked toward the sea. What they call the jewel box was glittering between the foothills and the coast. It was still just light enough to make out the shore, the dark hulk of

39

Catalina, and the blinking lights on an airliner that had just taken off. I moved a chair around so I could face it, having once, as a poet, compelled myself to sit and stare at what I considered beautiful. It's impossible. Try it sometime. If the sight really moves you, the first thing you do is turn away. That's how, I would say, we know that it's beautiful. We can't really cope with the sensation except to turn away and talk about it, but I had once made the effort, years ago, on the isle of Capri. The view across toward Naples, or south toward Sorrento, is of that sort. Something in the mind lights up, then blacks out, at the sight of it. I sat there all afternoon, staring, but when I think of Capri right now what I see are the views in my Uncle Clyde's stereopticon library. It is still intact. Vesuvius wears its immortal plume. A woman dressed like my mother gazes toward it from beneath her parasol.

I sat there thinking of that, and how I had turned from the sight of that wonderful girl the same way, having on my mind's eye nothing that I could call a picture of her. Over the loud-speaker system, which they had in every room, I could hear the ghostly rumble among the drums and the asthmatic whisper in the trombones that swung me back, just the way they did Fitzgerald, to a world that seemed obliged to get better and better in every way. Listening to the band it occurred to me that every sentiment had its own pitch, the way that every generation has its own sentiment. Good or bad. The pitch we hear today, the phony pitch, is absolutely right for the phony sex, the phony sentiment, and the phony mountain ballads poured out of the pine-scented plastic maple syrup cans. If you think that crime doesn't pay you haven't been to the movies lately, or checked the juvenile and senile delinquents on your local jukebox. The word for it is slobism. They grunt, groan, and grind, but seldom reach the level of speech. If I sound a little bitter, remember that I'm old enough to know better, but I'm paid according to how well I can forget what I know. The current crop of singers are medicine men and snake charmers. Everything is in the sales talk and nothing in what they sell. The phony pitch has to make up for what the song lacks. The pitch of Pussy Amor, singing one of our songs, is based entirely on the assumption that you have heard *better* songs, but at least this reminds you of one of them. I thought of all this because I was listening to one of the few songs I wish I had written, and I sat there, just the way Mac would have, crooning "Just One More Chance." I sang

41

the refrain, but it had been so long since I wanted another chance, I'd forgotten the words. The way Bing used to do it, I whistled. I finished off with the refrain—

"Just one more cha-ance . . ."

like I really meant it.

My drink was on the floor, I had this plate in my lap, and I sat there facing this view through the window— but the window itself, as I gazed, obstructed the view. In it I could see, clearly reflected, the girl who stood in the doorway behind me. The girl I had looked for. The one I doubted was real. She saw my own reflection in the window—she saw that I saw her now, and said:

"Just one more chance . . . what for?"

How long had she been there? I was certain that if I turned to look at her, she would disappear. As a rule I am handy with words, glib, you might say, but I said nothing. I gazed at her face—I tried, that is, to penetrate behind the impression, the one reflected in the glass, that she was beautiful. The face oval. The hair, I hardly thought of the color, in loose ringlets. The mouth—as I looked at her lips they slowly parted, as if to speak, but instead she raised the glass she was holding and took a sip. That was all, just moistening her lips, leaving

a cool film that made them shiny, and perhaps exagger-
ated the whiteness of her teeth. I'm a little uncertain
without my glasses, but whether it was her reflection or
the window that wavered, what I saw blurred in focus
and rippled like the shadows that water casts.

"Yes—?" I heard her say, as if expecting an answer.
Then I heard a voice in the hall calling, "Eva! Oh,
Eva!" and she turned away. I rose out of my chair
spilling the plate on the floor and kicking over my drink.
Behind her, through the door, I could see this big fellow
coming toward her with two plates.

"Look!" I heard myself say, and she wheeled around
toward me, took that flower from her hair, and as she
tossed it toward me said:

"—in case you want that chance."

The young fellow with her saw what she had done, and
they both laughed. I let the flower lie there while I
cleaned up the mess. I tossed it on the tray, with the
celery, the ice cubes, and the pieces of plate I had
broken, carrying them down the hall to where the dirty
dishes were stacked. In the dim light of the hall my hand
went out and picked off the flower. I slipped it into the
pocket of my coat, then stood in the main room, with
perhaps forty people, listening to an old lecher sing the

usual run of dirty songs. He got a big hand. At one point
I heard Mac shout, "That's great, man!"

I saw her twice. Looking for the men's room I saw her
seated on one of the landings, her back toward me, two
young men at her feet and her hand held by the one
seated at her side. I was relieved to see their fingers were
not laced. Then, an hour later, looking for Mac, I saw
her reflected in a cloakroom mirror, running a comb
through her hair, her strong brown arms raised above
her head. That was where I recognized it. I may have
said it aloud. The word *Greek*. One without the mutila-
tions. One with all the limbs intact.

I would have gone at that point rather than see who
would be holding her hand on the next landing, but I
couldn't go off without Mac. You may find it hard to
believe that a man of thirty-eight, who flies his own air-
plane, neither drives nor has the nerve to drive a car.
I couldn't leave him to a cab, since I'm never sure he
knows where he lives. I asked one of the caterers if they
had a piano, and he replied that they did, in what he
called the playroom, and, as I might have expected, Mac
was there. So were fifteen or twenty other people, listening to him. He loves old upright pianos, and he has this
idea they go with his music. They don't. But he loves the

idea. He had been trying some of our new stuff on them, and this little Southern chick, with her big damp voice, was talking the words I had put into her mouth.

"What next?
The life of love I knew
No longer loves
The things I do.
What next?"

If the test of a song is what it stands up under, this was a good song. She got a hand from the crowd, and she was set to run through the few little things she knew, which would have been plenty, but I stepped forward at that point and raised my hand. The answer to "What Next?" I said, was that I had to take its composer, the gent seated at the keyboard, home so he could finish the song. We had just three verses, I said, and it called for four. Then, to make this little chick feel good, I made a few remarks about our new songbird, and how much her style brought back the old days of Fanny Brice.

Nobody laughed when I said that. They gave us all a big hand. There you have the new show business in a nutshell. You tell them what they're going to like, they like it, then they all stand and applaud themselves. In the

45

general happy hubbub I got Mac away from the piano, grabbed hold of the girl, and got them to the stairs. I kept my eye peeled for the Greek, but she was gone. Some prankster had propped up a poster of Rin Tin Tin in the back seat of our car, lifelike as hell in the moonlight, and I just left it there and drove off. We drove this little chick back to her apartment, where Mac kissed her chastely on the forehead, then let me wait five or ten minutes while she looked for her keys.

Driving west along Sunset, cruising through the blinkers and coming out above the lights, on some of the rises, kept the feeling that was building up in me from being localized. Not till I parked the car, came in through the back, and made Mac his usual nightcap of whisky—not till I had one myself, a little stiffer than usual, did it all come back. I hadn't eaten. I felt squeamish and a little sick.

"Whassamatta?" Mac said, dunking his cubes, the way he likes to, with his finger.

"Must be something I ate," I said, which he didn't question, since that often happened.

Our bedroom is at the top front of this mansion, from where you can view the sea in the morning, but I could hear Mac, after I had gone to bed, hammering the baby

46

grand. Like everybody in the world, he likes to play Rachmaninoff. I lay there thinking, of one thing and another, and when it was clear I was not going to sleep I got out of bed and looked in my pocket for that paper flower. I stepped into the bathroom, closing the door, to examine it. I know nothing about flowers. This one had white petals you could pluck off. I plucked off several, then I noticed that one petal seemed to have a serial number. I could see very plainly the number 2-8117. I could not make out the letters that preceded it. It was slow to dawn on me that what I had was a phone number. Part of one, that is. We have about a dozen telephones in the place, but it took me half an hour to find a phone book, then another half-hour to grasp the problem. I had no exchange. Thirty-two were listed in the general Los Angeles area.

What did I know about the girl?

Her name was Eva. That was not very much.

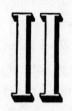

My mother used to say to me, "Earl, you've got to eat to live."

I usually start the day with bacon and eggs, some fresh or stewed fruit, three or four slices of toast, then a pint of strong coffee I brew in an espresso I carry around.

I had a glass of orange juice. I poured it, that is, but I could hardly get it down. But to live you have to eat, and since I wanted to live I took one of Mac's diet crackers, two of his vitamin pills, and then went in search of a phone. A private phone. I might have to put in some thirty-odd calls.

I began with the A's. Women invariably answered the phone. I would ask for Eva and they would tell me that I had the wrong number. As a rule, of course, the operator told me that first. You have dialed the wrong number, she would say. We got to know each other very well. "Did you try Superior?" she suggested at one point. So I tried Superior. That was not it, but it took me up farther in the alphabet. I dialed Vandyke, a small child answered, and in a routine way I asked for Eva. "Just a sec—" the child replied, then she turned from the phone and screamed:

"Ohhhhhhh, EEEEE-vaaaaa."

The next thing I knew there she was.

"Hello?" she said.

My mouth was dry. Was this the one? "Hello," I said.

"I was wondering when you would call," she said.

"If *who* would call?" I said. "Which one am I?"

"You want another chance," she said, "don't you?"

"Yes," I replied.

"At what?"

"At you," I said.

Only now as I write it down do I see how corny it is. At the time it struck me as wonderful. I suppose I hoped it would bowl her over, since I was quite aware that it didn't. I could hear a child yelling.

"Are they all yours?" I said.

She laughed. "I suppose they are mine."

"You suppose?"

"I'm a governess."

A minute may have passed. I had time to read, four or five times, the Fire and Police warnings on the directory.

"Hello?" she said.

"You seem to have your hands full—already," I said.

"It's a job," she replied. "Doesn't everybody?"

"I'm sorry," I said, then I blurted it out. "I found this phone number, my dear, and I don't remember having asked for it."

That set her back. I fully expected her to hang up. I could hear that child in the background—that doll-like wheeze of very young babies—and I don't know why I didn't hang up myself. It flashed through my mind that this girl had a husband, a house full of brats, and Christ knows what all in one of those lovely new developments you see springing up. Running an orphanage by day, and playing Mamie Stover by night.

"I'm just so damn poohed," she said. "I got in so late."

"I'm sorry," I said. "I really am. I—"

"I've got the baby right now," she interrupted. "He wants to be fed. You want to call me back about eleven o'clock?"

"Sure," I replied. "Sure, at eleven." Then she either hung up or someone on another phone in the same house cut us off. I sat there. I made note of the Vandyke exchange. Then I got up and came back to the kitchen where Mac was soft-boiling himself three eggs.

"You feel any better, man?"

"I think so," I said. But I could see that I didn't look it.

"There somethin' on your mind?" he said.

It occurred to me that there was. "Christ!" I said. If you have lived through a war with somebody and then tied your habits of living and dying up with him, it hardly matters what sort of a boob he actually is.

"What's wrong, man?"

"I forgot to ask her name," I replied.

He rocked the saucepan with the eggs in it, something I've told him a thousand times didn't help any, then he turned and said:

"How you like Billie? Ain't she some chick?"

I could see that he thought so. When I said the same to him, I knew what it was I wanted to hear.

"You're a lucky slob," I said. Nothing pleased him more than to hear he was a slob—but a lucky one. It braced him up enough so he could put to me the big one.

"Think she's got a talent?" he said.

If he'd said voice, he would have had me. But a talent she had. Look what she had done with it.

"That chick's going to go a long way," I said, and weak as I was, my voice carried conviction. He felt it.

"She's got sumpin', man. You know what I mean?"

I sure did. I was looking at it. She had it, all right, and the question was what would she be doing with it.

I filled two of our thermos jugs with iced coffee, took along some zwieback to keep myself alive, and we headed for the beach. I needn't tell you who we found camped smack on our spot. Miss Billie Harcum, with fresh nail polish where she had chipped it off her toes, wearing a trim little tank suit that did a good deal to improve her voice. Along with her was a tall, cool drink of water from the Veronica Lake period, one of the chicks who couldn't face up to a date with a man of forty-one. Miss Harcum introduced her to me in the nice quiet way that indicated I was a man finally faced with his destiny, and this chick played it cool in the way they had both mapped it out. I just happen to have a peculiar distaste for the fashionable phase in female contours, even when, as in this instance, it was nicely tanned. The fact that I was one shade darker than she was drew us

52

together for two or three minutes, plus the information that my cigarettes made her think of Caporal Bleus. We did France and Spain once over lightly so she could slide quickly into Mallorca, where Robert Graves had been the turning point in her life. That *too,* strangely enough, had been on the beach. He had asked one of their mutual friends "who that Cretan sort of creature was," and of course it had been her.

Since Mac had never heard of Robert Graves this story didn't catch fire the way it should have, and I think the word "Cretan" seriously troubled him. The one he knows, they spell with an i, I think. It being ten to eleven at that point, I excused myself, in a professional manner, and walked back to the corner of Sunset Boulevard to make my call. The drugstore there had a public telephone, but very public, behind the drug counter, and I had to stand where the woman at the fountain could listen to me. I put the call through, and it was Eva who answered.

"What an awful day," she said, before I could say anything. I could hear the sound of her breath in the mouthpiece, as if she had run to catch the phone.

"It's a beauty down here at the beach," I said, but I didn't mean it the way she took it.

"That's very interesting," she replied.

"Except for one little thing," I added.

She got that, all right, but it didn't seem to impress her.

"There's always some little thing," she said, then cupped her hand over the mouthpiece, but not before this child she was holding let out a howl. It left me deaf in that ear for a second or two. When I could hear again I said:

"It is now seven minutes past eleven, and I have just walked half a mile to put in this call."

That is what a howling kid does to me. If she had hung up, and she might have, I would have died.

"I'm just so damn poohed," she said. "If I just hadn't gone to that party—"

"I wouldn't be calling you," I said. She covered the mouthpiece again, and I could hear her pass the child to someone. I had only one dime along with me and my time was running out. "When am I going to see you?" I said.

"I get an hour off about three o'clock."

"You get *what*?"

"Forty-five minutes, but I might stretch it to an hour."

I took a deep breath, said, "Where will I meet you?"

Aloud she said, "Let me think," the way a woman

does who finds it a help to state the problem like that.

"Just remember I'm on a pay phone," I said.

"You know the campus?"

"What campus?"

"The UCLA campus."

"I can find it, I guess," I said.

"I'll be on the corner of Westwood and LeConte. It's a main corner. I'll be on the west side."

"At three?"

"I take the kids to a matinee which begins at two forty-five. I should make it by three."

"Okay," I said, "three o'clock," just as the phone chime rang in my ear, and the operator told me my time was up.

I've no idea whether I believed a word of that or not. I stood there till the woman at the soda fountain asked me if there was something I wanted, and I said no, then I changed my mind and asked for a glass of milk. I had to eat to live, and I still wanted to live. It took me five or ten minutes to force down that milk. Then I walked the quarter mile back to camp, where they had all moved in under Mac's umbrella and were listening to Pussy Amor sing her version of "What Next?"

"She's not too bad," Mac said, as I walked up, "but you're *great*!"

They made room for me and I asked these chicks if they knew how to get to the UCLA campus. They did. It was not far from where they lived. I said they would have to excuse me, a little later, since I had an important appointment, but I would be back to pick Mac up about five. That suited Miss Harcum to a T, but not her girl friend. The less interest I showed—and I doubt if it was possible to show less interest—the more this girl seemed to feel I was just her type. "While you were gone," Miss Harcum said, "you know what Nina said?" I didn't. "She said why didn't I tell her you were the Leslie Howard type."

"We're in about the same age bracket," I replied.

"As if that's what I meeeeeeaaaannnnnn!" said this chick.

Ordinarily I'm a great one for this kind of banter, but I felt almost too weak to talk. Don't ask me why. That is merely a statement of how I felt. I was forty-one years of age and had just made an appointment to see for less than an hour a girl who was more than likely just half that age. What for? I wanted to see if she was *real*. Not that that was entirely why—but I really did. I felt completely unreal myself. The thought that I might die, or faint away, before three o'clock came along led me to open a thermos and drink some black coffee. I couldn't just sit there, so I asked this chick if she felt like a walk. She did. I suppose she thought that this was her break. I led her down to where the sand was firm, then walked her more than a mile, all the way to Venice, then back again, without saying a word. It impressed her to beat hell. But favorably. Even on Mallorca she hadn't run into anything like that. When we got within a yell of our umbrella she suddenly broke away, like a kid, and ran that knock-kneed girlish run across the sand.

"You won't be-leevut," she said, "but we went all the way without a word! I've never done anything so thrilling in all my life."

They all watched me walk up, look at my wrist watch, then say that it was time for me to run along. That impressed her too. But not so favorably.

Some instinct I've learned to trust led me to drive back to our mansion, force down a banana, then brush my teeth with chlorophyll paste. I was still about half an hour early when I located the Westwood corner, so I parked a block to the east and just sat in the car. All she had to do was not show up. I sat there, listening to the radio, watching these good-looking sun-tanned kids, some of them in their forties, come and go until ten past three o'clock. I'd made up my mind to call it quits at three fifteen. Right at that point a roadster, with four in the front seat, pulled over sharp just ahead of me, and two of the boys rolled aside to let this girl out. Eva. She stood there a moment adjusting her skirt. Those boys blocked the traffic, ogling and talking, till the honking behind them made them move, and when the light changed to green she walked across the street. Just watching her walk I could hardly stand it. My hands shook. Two or three cars of college boys whistled and waved at her before I got my car started, and I was nearly sick with the thought that one of them would pick her up. But she was still there when I got there. When I stopped she got in. I turned off to the right at the next block just to get out of the stream of traffic, and heard her say:

"It looks like thirty minutes is all I've got."

I said, "You feel like a drink?"

"I really don't like to drink," she said.

"I tell you—" I said, bright as a kid, "why don't we just drive up to our place and park. It's quiet."

When I said that, she made her first move. Toward

58

the door. She pulled over to it and hung one brown arm out. I was so ashamed I could have cried, but I couldn't tell a girl who looked like a bombshell that all I wanted to do was just go somewhere and look at her.

"Which way?" I said, as we were back on Sunset. What I meant at the time was which way to get her home.

"*A gauche*," she said, wagging her hand at the wrist, which was the first little tag end of sophistication. At the next turn she said, "*A droite*," and I pulled into a coffee shop parking lot. I started to open my door, when she said:

"Is this one of those tops that come up?"

I didn't know. We had been given the car with the top down, and that was how I had left it. She leaned over and examined the dashboard, flicked a switch, and up came the top. Out of the back, like a phantom, it rose up behind us like a hood, then dropped. The front seat was suddenly dark and quiet as a cave.

"Why don't we just sit?" she said, and took a cigarette from her purse. I watched her light it, draw on it, and when she settled back into the corner, blue as a fish bowl through the cloud of smoke, I saw her eyes. They held my gaze. She did not ask me why I was staring at her. She did not ask me what was on my mind.

Her eyes held my gaze until the lids, as if the effort suddenly fatigued them, slowly closed, lowering my own gaze to her lips. They were parted. A fleck of cigarette paper held my eye. One of her front teeth had come in with a twist and smoking had given it a yellow cast. The ivory color, I remember thinking, of an old piano key. She did not speak, but feeling my gaze she sucked the lower lip into her mouth, and made a sound in her throat like a cat awakened with a stroke of the hand. Without opening her eyes she rocked toward me, the cigarette fell on the seat between us, and I crushed it with my knee as I rocked toward her. I did not kiss her. I fastened on her lips. Whatever impulse the vampire has to fasten on flesh and draw life from it, I shared with him, and she seemed to share with me. A car pulled in on our left, one backed out on our right, a drive-in waitress took and delivered orders, leaving her tray to rock on the fender of our car. I was the first to draw away, and she said:

"It's time, isn't it?"

I saw that it was. I started the car, and driving back to Westwood she arranged her face in the rearview mirror, combed her hair, and put back the lipstick I had wiped off. With the tip of her Kleenex she removed some

of it from my face. I let her out of the car a block east of
the movie where she had left the kids at the matinee. She
turned and said:

"You want to call me at eight?"

"I'll call," I said.

I watched her go down the street past a parking lot
where two young men hailed her, one of them eating
ice cream, and he came forward with his sandwich and
gave her a bite. Together, they walked on down to the
corner, where the doors of the movie were opening, and
they stood there chatting till the kids she had to take
home came along.

I didn't drive right back to the beach. I drove up the
canyon to our place, where I walked into the bathroom
and looked at the mirror, not seeing for a moment the
red stain around my mouth. Otherwise the tan concealed
how I really looked. The house was cool, but a film of
perspiration beaded my lips. I took several of the barbital tablets that Mac keeps on hand for a TV performance, then I set the alarm for six o'clock and lay down
on the couch. I wondered if a woman agreeably raped
felt as I felt. I just wondered. The idea did cross my
mind. Little else, neither pleasure nor pain, except for

the delight of the flavor, slightly perfumed, that her lips had left in my mouth. I had not closed my eyes before the alarm went off. I took a shower, ate three spoonfuls of the cottage cheese we keep in the icebox, brushed my teeth, changed my shirt, and drove down to the beach. Mac and his chick were there, very cozy, but the girl friend had gone. She had a course in speech projection at seven o'clock.

The day before, I would have done what I could to protect Mac from himself, but now I suggested that we all go to some quiet place and eat. I couldn't bear the thought of eating, but if I got *them* fed and settled down for the evening, I'd be free at eight o'clock.

We drove along the shore to a place in Malibu, where we had a drink at the bar, then sat at a table where Miss Harcum could admire the sea. I usually gaze into a woman's eyes, being a successful song-and-dance man, but I'd picked up this habit in the last few hours of looking at the mouth. The more I looked at Miss Harcum's mouth—when it was closed and I could look at it—the more it seemed like a horn player's solo in a tight little string ensemble. It didn't go. It just didn't belong with the face. The moment my eyes settled on her lips I had the unpleasant sensation that I was seeing something she didn't know was exposed. Her mouth is what you'd call full, in the attractive sense, but the upper lip had a tuck in it, a little row of pleats, as if she was tasting a lemon peel. She had it painted to match her nails, and do something interesting with her tan, but the one impression I got was that it was *raw*.

My condition being what it was, undernourished on the one hand, and overstimulated on the other, I didn't take these observations too seriously. But it did lead me to turn and look at the mouths around the candlelight beside us, just the big red mouths, and it gave me quite a start. I mean it gave me the weemies. So many sets of sharp teeth in a purse of flesh. I had a period as a kid when all I saw in a woman's face was her nose, and I don't recommend you have a try at something like that. All you see, after a little practice, are the holes in the face. Now all I saw was lips, the hardness of the lips the moment the mouth closed, like a flytrap, then sprang open like an evil toy to show you the teeth. Something you fed. Something you had to *keep* fed, that is. You pressed the little button, the jaws spread wide, then you dropped something in to keep it mollified. You either did, bygod, or the mouth looked out for itself. It prowled, like a sleepwalker, around the house at night.

It was not just a part of the face, as we think, but the major entrance to the body—the rest of the face was there merely to make sure that the mouth got fed. The eyes were there, you might say, to see the prey, then lure it within reach. I'm not just elaborating on a gruesome notion but trying to tell you how I felt, sitting there in this fishhouse, watching this group of lovely female mouths. I'm not excluding males. It just so happens that the females interest me. My own mouth, frankly, often scares the hell out of me. It also naturally crossed my mind that I had just come, almost within the hour, from feeding on lips that must resemble these. I am forty-one. I do not easily kid myself. If something had come over me during the day that I could not explain in terms of normal behavior, it did not deprive me of drawing certain conclusions about mouths. A pretty little painted, tainted, scented pocket cannibal.

The moment we had taken a seat in this place Miss Harcum referred to me as Uhl, honey; to Mac, as Macky, honey; and to the kid who cleaned the table as just plain honey, but with sugar on it. She kept up this flow of southern sunshine, asking the busboy wheah he was from, the waitress wheah she got that wonnaful hairdo, and so forth. I suppose it reflected how much out of water she felt. Here she had this famous song writer, Irwin Macgregor, on her clean little hands. Did she want him? I could see that she did if he would just keep his own little hands where they belonged.

Anyhow, that was how I sized up Miss Harcum, a great one to gaze at you through a cloud of smoke, but tight as a button if your knees happened to rub. The clothespin school, as Mac calls them, with reference to their thighs, but if they happen to be clothespins he found in a dime store, why then it's all right. No, it's more than all right. Man, it's great.

When Mac is in love—when he is in, that is, the condition I have just described—my battle-scarred slob of a song writer is a boy at heart. He blushes at the word "honey," and wriggles like a seal at a glance from her eyes. I've learned to marvel at and professionally respect this sort of thing. A first-class second-rate song hit-of-the-month will come out of it. Third-class pop songs are all written by the boys who know better than to believe their own nonsense, but the good stuff is still turned out by the boob who believes in it. When the right sort of chick comes along, Mac can believe.

"It's got to have heart, man!" he says. "You know what I mean?" And I do.

In between short runs at his bouillabaisse he managed to coin a handful of words that I could paste together into a sentence for his light o' love. He wanted to take her home and give her a try on the tape. If she sounded as good on the tape as she had the night before, in the rumpus room, if she sounded even half that good, he would give her a chance. We would, that is. I would put the words of love into her mouth. We would darken her up and give her a cute little Mexican part. Some chic little *Camino Real* sort of thing. None of that exactly depressed her, and while she dabbed around in her lobster—the hardware they gave her was something new —I drank the tomato juice cocktail that Mac hadn't touched. *Tempus* fidgets, as you know, and at seven forty-five I stepped back to the phone.

I got one of those damn kids again, one just learning about the phone, and more interested in saying something clever than listening. The word "Eva" didn't seem to click with him. The little bastard kept repeating, "This tha Mattson resituns." Then she must have heard him; I heard a scuffle, and she said:

"Hello?"

"Hello, Greek," I said.

If your condition is right, you can use the telephone

like a stethoscope. Mine was. I could hear the intake of her breath when I said Greek. I hadn't been aware of it at the time, but now I could see, right where I could touch it, the pulse beat in the flesh at her throat.

"Say something," I said.

"Can you come at nine?"

"Come where?"

"Here."

"Where is *here*?"

"Oh—" she said, then she told me to go down Sunset to Kentwood, make a right turn, then a left, then follow that road up the canyon till it stopped. I can't explain it, but the way she did it I knew I wasn't the first one to have asked that question. Just to keep her on the phone I repeated the directions.

"I've got to go now," she said, and hung up.

When Kafka struck on the telephone as the symbol of modern man's frustration, I would be willing to bet it had something to do with a chick. One minute you have her, then you don't. It suddenly crossed my mind that I still didn't know her name.

I bought a pack of cigarettes, then went back to the table and said that it was now eight o'clock, so I had to get back and dress for an appointment I had at nine.

That suited Mac fine, but I could see Miss Harcum make a quick run through everything her mother had told her. But when life comes at you in a fishhouse, you either take it or duck. She decided to take it.

"Uhl, honey, you be shoh yoh get me home uhly now?"

I said that I would.

In this fire engine I've already described, we drove along the coast highway to Sunset, arousing the envy and concern of the Thunderbird couples that went by. It gave the bad-taste monster I was driving a certain class. Only Trader Horn, some oil mogul, or the kingpin in the new white-slave traffic would ride around in a squad car with the siren turned off. Billie Harcum loved it. Her pretty little pony tail whipped in the wind. Driving very slow gets you the notice today that driving very fast once did, and we had all the attention we could use going back. Miss Harcum was naturally impressed with our layout, but not so impressed as she might have been, since she was too young to have learned about culture from Citizen Kane. It was pure dog, but she missed the finer touch. Pure dog is nothing without the mothball scent of nostalgia.

I made them some drinks before changing my clothes, and put a stack of our songs on the record player. I felt a little sorry for Miss Harcum—but not too much. All of Mac's ideas of a *soirée intime* come from the French novels he has never read but thought he heard somebody or other tell him about. The wolf wears a kimono and sprays himself with eau de cologne. Mac varies the classical routine by slipping on a crucifix with garnets, and smoking Turkish cigarettes in a holder imported from France. He excused himself to get into his outfit, and I got into mine.

What outfit? Did she want me to take her to a place like Ciro's or something with class? If she liked to dance, we would go somewhere and dance. I picked out a modified summer formal, of the type I had seen around Las Vegas, and the effect was pretty handsome with my tan. For the third or fourth time in the last five hours I brushed my teeth. Mac was still in the shower when I had finished, so I told Miss Harcum to make herself at home. To give the place a cool professional air I set up the sound tape near the piano, and gave her a few pointers as to how to pitch her voice to the mike. It wasn't lost on me, in this discussion, that she thought her voice would be better if I was around to listen to it, instead of Mac. Not that I was flattered. It just so happens that Mac scares the hell out of them—and I don't. This judgment, as I say, is not flattering. I said I was sure her voice would be lovely and could hardly wait to get back to hear it, which would probably be around eleven o'clock. I knew I wouldn't, but that was what I said.

I found Kentwood where the Greek said it would be, made the turns she told me to take, then wound up the grade for about a mile to this place at the top. The road wheeled around a flower bed at the turn, then passed through a big gate into a courtyard. Nothing pretentious, just a big, plain comfortable-looking place: out in back a garden of the odorless flowers they grow in profusion out here, glowing with the artificial brightness of candle wax. Two or three of the kids I had seen at the movie were kicking a ball around the yard, but when I came up the drive they turned and hollered at the house. The Greek came out of a door at the side. She was wearing something simple—she knew about *that*—and she carried this child saddled on her hip, held very casually in the crook of her arm. She came toward me, smiling, this child on her haunch, and if I had been standing my knees would have buckled. Every cliché in the world once had its moment of truth. At some point, if you traced it back, it expressed the inexpressible, and I was face to face with the original Madonna and Child. Not even her own, just any child would do, and being a precocious, gifted child one of his grubby little hands was fondling her breast. She came to the door of the car and said:

"I've got to hold him till he burps," and with the first finger of her free hand she cleaned the food from his gums, sniffed it on her finger, then wiped the finger clean on the diaper he wore. That gesture, that kind of knowledge, cut through the self-awareness of the pose, and I knew what it was that paralyzed me about this girl. Life without its clichés. Vegetable, animal, and mineral.

"It won't be long now," she said, matter-of-factly, and wheeled slowly around—she is a big girl—and with the walk that a big Lachaise bronze would have had, crossed the yard to the house. She was gone until the yard had almost darkened, then she came out. I opened the door and she took a seat in the car. I turned around in the drive, went out through the gate, and at the flower bed curve to the road the last of the light from the sky streamed into the car. I slowed to a stop, turned to look at her face. She held my gaze until I said:

71

"Greek, close your eyes," and she closed them. Like a man testing glasses that he doubted, I stared at her mouth. The lips were parted. I could feel the coolness of her teeth. Never in my life had I seen anything so beautiful. Never in my life had I felt anything so desirable. "You can open your eyes," I said, and when she did I examined her eyes. My throat was dry. I had to wet my lips before I could speak.

"What would you like to do?" I said, and saw on her face, amused but softly melancholy, the Mona Lisa smile.

"Is there anything else?" she said, and I moved my raincoat out of the seat, drew her over closer to my side. I put the car in neutral, let it drift down the grade. At the corner of Sunset, I said:

"Any particular place?"

"Any place."

So we drove west on Sunset to the sea, as it has been done in ten thousand phony movies, a million phony songs, and twice that many mortgaged cars. For the second time that day I took the coast highway to Malibu. Just beyond Malibu, on a rise, where a row of cabins had a view of the sea, I pulled in under a sign that said OFFICE. A man came out.

"We are in love," I said, "and want something good."

The freshness of the cliché disarmed him. He winked at me, wiggled his finger, and I followed him down to a cabin at the front, a window on the sea, a bed, and a fireplace. To give it charm it was strewn with shells and driftwood, and hung with strips of net. I tipped him well to indicate that it was beautiful. He watched, through the curtains at his window, while I led the girl along the walk, and I tortured him unnecessarily by taking our time. As we stepped inside the door she stopped and kicked off her high-heeled shoes.

Some love stories stop right there, others start. This one moved imperceptibly into a quieter gear. Our cabin contained shells, fish nets, strips of wood, a lamp, a table, a bathroom, and a bed. No chairs. A simple facing up to the facts.

I hung my clothes on the hooks behind the door and she tossed hers, as they came off, on the bed. One of the shoes she had kicked off at the door had landed there. There was still a bright afterglow in the sky, and it cast her shadow on the wood floor. A big shadow. I was able to undress in the shade of it. We both stripped down like people who were anxious for a dip before the pool

73

closed, saying nothing, just getting duds off and out of the way. She was tanned all over, I mean all over, the way Madame Monroe is blonde all over, and I was so struck by it that I said:

"How the devil did you manage?"

She turned to see what I meant.

"Oh—" she said, "I just swim out to the rocks."

I didn't doubt it. She was built like something intended to float. I could almost see her, through our window, floating like a raft in that wild blue yonder with her nose, her toes, and the nipples of her breasts showing. She looked at me, carefully, and indicated that what she saw was all right. I suppose every man has a dream of being like Adam and Eve with a woman, without shame or embarrassment, and that's how it was. I looked at her lovingly and said:

"How did you do that?"

She looked down her front to see what I saw, and ran the tips of her fingers along the scar. It looked to be about eight inches along, up the center of her abdomen.

"I nearly died," she said.

"An accident?" I said, knowing that it wasn't.

"A Caesarean," she replied, and went into the bathroom. She came back for her plastic handbag, then went in again. I stood at the window, gazing at the rocks, the Sargasso Sea of kelp near the shore, and then farther out to sea where just a week before I had seen a whale spout. A man on the beach had suddenly leaped up, shouted, "Thar she blows!" But nobody had believed it. If he had hollered "flying saucers" there would have been ten thousand witnesses. In the bathroom I could hear the water running and the scrubbing sound of a brush on her teeth. When it stopped I said:

"I want to tell you that I haven't really eaten since I first saw you. I haven't slept, and my knees will bend both ways."

"Does it matter?" she replied.

"I may not give a good account of myself."

"You're a man, not a boy," she said, matter-of-factly. "You'll do all right."

If she hadn't said that I very much doubt it. I state it as a simple fact. She came out of the bathroom without her bag and walked to where she stood right before me. Without her high-heeled shoes our eyes were level, our lips were exactly level, and when I kissed her she put an arm around me as if to hold me up. Then she drew away and said:

"I've got to get back by twelve o'clock."

I had left on my wrist watch, which I then took off and gave the stem a few winds before putting it on the table. It was five past ten. Light from the rising moon cast shadows on the beach. She was lying with her eyes closed when I turned, so relaxed there was something unearthly about her, so much at peace she seemed dead and on the other side of what we call life. I stood a moment looking at her parted lips.

"You'll do all right," she said, as if to reassure me, but her fears were unfounded. I mean my fears. I was a man and not a boy—as she said—and I did all right.

I had the fingers of one hand, when I woke up, in the curls at the scruff of her neck. Gripped. The way a cat lugs a kitten around the house. The way you might do it in a dream, I began to laugh. I don't know whether she had been asleep or just lying there, relaxed and waiting, but when my diaphragm began to bob she began to laugh too. No questions or answers. We just lay there and laughed. I had never before been with a woman who could bear my amusement without questioning, let alone the humor of a man who had just been lying with her. She didn't care. We lay there and laughed like a crazy pair of kids. When it had died down, naturally, I said:

"Not that it matters, but what is your name? I might need to know it sometime."

"Baum," she replied.

"Baum?"

"Tree," she said, "in German."

"I'll call you Greek," I said. "Is that all right?"

"I like it."

"My name is Earl Horter," I said, hoping she would have something else to call me. But she didn't.

"Earl Horter," she said, repeating the words. That was all.

"I'm a writer of lyrics," I said, thinking she might have heard the name. "You see it on sheet music. You might have seen it in movies sometimes."

I thought that might impress her. She didn't seem to care.

"I don't have time for movies," she replied.

I was about to say something, then didn't. Wasn't it plain enough where her time went?

"How old are you?"

"Twenty-three."

"I will be forty-one in September." I waited for her to say that I didn't look it. She said:

"Is that all? You are lean and wiry like older men."

77

I am—but I am still human. I closed my eyes and she said:

"Are you married?"

"No. Are you?"

Her head wagged from side to side on my arm. Then she said, "I was once. I was married at fourteen."

"Fourteen?"

"Oh, I was old enough," she replied.

I could believe it.

"When I was fifteen I nearly died. The child was turned wrong in the tube. I was dead. They said I was dead and came back to life."

Something like a tremor passed through my body and she turned, pulled the sheet up on me, "You cold?"

I shook my head, then said, "No." She turned on her elbow and looked at my face in the dark. I could see the pearl in the ring she wore at her ear. "If you had died—" I said, "you wouldn't be here." She made that purring sound in her throat, the sound she had made just before I kissed her. "Is that why you are?" I said.

"What?"

"Here," I said, and gripped her by the scruff.

"When I'm afraid—" she began.

"You afraid?"

"Oh, I'm often afraid. But when I'm afraid I tell myself I was once dead."

"That gives you courage?"

"This life I have is a gift," she said. "Why should I hoard it? I have a life to give."

I cannot tell you about her voice. It is like trying to tell you about a new flavor, like a mango, for instance.

"You don't like that?"

I kissed her. After the kiss I said, "I'm lean and wiry. I have only one life. I am a selfish and hungry middle-aged man. I don't like to hear about all you have to give."

"But if I *have* it to give—"

"Love—" I said, but went no further. What, after all, did I know about love? In a cabin just north of Malibu I lay in bed with a girl whose name I had just learned. What did I want? I wanted to lie there with her every night. I wanted to keep what I had found all to myself.

"You do not sleep with girls?" she asked.

"Greek—" I began, "what time is it?"

She held up her wrist so I could see the watch.

"It is twenty past eleven," I said. She pushed up, yawning. I heard her scratch a bite on her leg. "In answer to your question," I went on, "I do not sleep with

79

girls to make *them* happy. When I feel a great desire, as I do with you, then I sleep with them if I can." I stopped, then added, "But it's been damn seldom in forty-one years."

"If you had died," she replied, "you would feel different." She threw back the sheet and sat on the edge of the bed. I lay there watching her put her clothes back on. When she stood up to put on her bra I could see the white cups against her dark skin, and I rose up in bed to reach for her, pull her back down.

"You can see how much will power I have," I said.

She pushed me away and said, "But that *is* will power. The mind is in the body."

The phrase she had used, coming when it did, almost made me laugh. I was glad it was dark and she could not see the expression on my face.

"So the mind is in the body?"

"It is in yours and mine," she replied, which I liked to hear, then she added, "and a lot of other people who don't seem to know it," which I didn't like. "Hurry up," she said, matter-of-factly, "I can't be late."

I got up and slipped on my pants. "You like this job?"

"It's a job, and I don't want to lose it."

"You looked mighty professional," I said. She didn't

bother to reply. In the bathroom I could hear her splashing water on her face. When she came back into the room I said:

"What did you do before this—?"

"School. I've just finished four years of college."

In a woman like that it seems strange when the girl speaks up.

"What did you major in?" I asked, curious.

"Music. I play the piano."

I wondered if I'd heard that right, then said, "Did you hear me say I was a song writer?"

"I'm serious," she said. "I play the classics."

While I finished dressing she sat on the bed and smoked.

"What do you plan to do?" I said. She didn't answer right away, and I added, "With yourself."

"Something always turns up."

"That's not much of a plan, is it?"

"You can't plan your development," she replied.

I had stepped into the bathroom to comb my hair. I stood there facing the mirror. I'm sensitive to the word *development*. Meaning to kid her a little I said:

"What part of your development am I?"

"I suppose I'm tired of boys," she replied.

I let the water run for a spell, then I said:

"Got all they have to give, is that it?"

"I don't know," she said. "I just know I'm tired."

I came back into the room and put on my shirt and coat. I felt cheated and ashamed. When I slipped on my coat I felt in the inside pocket for my billfold. The empty room, the mussed-up bed, the rafters garlanded with nets that looked like cobwebs, suddenly looked fake.

"Is there any little thing," I said, "that I did that these boys couldn't do?"

I wanted to hurt her, I suppose, the way she had hurt me. I stood near the window, my hand held to my chest as I strapped on my wrist watch, the pale light from the sky on the face and the silver band. When she didn't reply I turned to look at her, just the outline of her head and shoulders. The hand resting on the bed at her side held the glowing cigarette. Although I could not see her face I felt her steady gaze. "Is there?" I repeated, certain that there wasn't.

"You arouse my desire," she said.

In the floor of the cabin I could feel the pounding of the surf. I had set my eyes on a light, a planet perhaps, to the north of Catalina, on the rim of the sea.

"I suppose that's not to be sneezed at, is it?" I said.

She made no comment. Her cigarette glowed brightly as she inhaled, then she dropped it on the floor and stepped on it. I walked to the door and let the light from the driveway stream in. Several cars besides our own were now parked out in front.

As she went ahead of me down the walk I noticed the lint from the diaper on her hip, and in the heel of her right stocking a large hole. Is this the Million-Dollar Baby, new style, I thought? I gave her my hand on the flight of stairs, and she did not draw away. By the time I had walked around the car, lit a cigarette, and slid in behind the wheel, she had climbed in and turned the radio on. She dialed it to a station playing the classics. Rachmaninoff. The pathos of the moment—diaper lint and the classics—the part-time lovers riding home in the moonlight, left such a staleness in my mouth I was almost sick. The thirty minutes it took to drive back we did not speak. At one point she said, "Why do you drive so slow?" and I had to sit and think about it. I thought, then said:

"I eat ice cream slow. I put off the best bite of everything to the last. I go slow to taste it longer, I suppose."

"I don't," she replied.

Up near the end of that road where she lived she suddenly said, "Stop here," and I stopped. She opened the door on her side and let herself out. When she turned to close it without slamming I caught her eye. There was just enough glow from the dashboard to light her face. She had not troubled to put on more lipstick and the scouring I had given her lips had left them almost puffy.

"Look, Greek—" I said, but when I leaned toward her she turned and ran, her heels clacking on the drive, her skirts lifted to the point where I could see her garters. Near the gate at the top she turned and said:

"Call me tomorrow," then she was gone.

I drove around for a while, aimlessly, then I went up the canyon to our place where the lights were still on and I could hear a piano tapping out "What Next?" I thought it might be the sound tape, but Mac was playing it himself. Miss Harcum was nowhere in sight, and I said:

"Well, how did things go?" which he didn't hear. A good sign. He never hears well when he's full of heart. The lid of the tape recorder was up and I could see they had run through a spool of the tape. "How's your new wren?" I said, since he refers to his new songbirds as little wrens. Without glancing at me he replied:

"Sent her home. She's got to get her rest."

The early nesting phase of Mac's love routine calls for nursing the little wren back to health. Early to bed, pasteurized milk, filter-tip cigarettes, that sort of thing. He surprised me by saying:

"She's great, man. You know what I mean?"

"You mean her talk on the tape?" I replied.

Mac has a smile, when he's full of heart, which expresses his pity for cynical people, people like myself, who have to get through life without the old pump.

"Like to hear a song or two?" he said, which was my cue for picking up the glasses, what was left of the bourbon, and heading for the back of the house. I was rinsing glasses when he came in and said:

"You feel better, man?"

"I don't feel too bad," I said.

"You get her name all right?"

I nodded. I so seldom show an interest in the girls that the one feeling he can localize is worry. Chicks break up great teams. He considered us a great team.

"Any name I might know?" he put in, and took an ice cube from one of the glasses, slipped it into his mouth, then crunched down on it. He knows what that does to me but it's a sure sign that he's worried.

"I'm turning in," I said, and crossed the hall to

where he keeps his barbital, took four of them, then went down the hall to our room.

"Look man!" I heard him say, and waited there in the hall until he came down and stood before me. "Now whassamatta?" he said.

"To think I picked it up from you."

"Look man—picked what?"

"Look!" I yelled. *"Look–look–look!"* Then I turned and walked into our bedroom. Two of the walls are glass and the room was full of the damn moonlight. For the second time that night I undressed in the dark. I must be the goddamnedest mimic in the world, since I stood in the center of the room, like she did, and tossed my clothes as I took them off on the foot of the bed.

"Why you so touchy, man?" Mac said through the door, and I lay in bed listening to him take a shower. He rubs into his hair a formula to prevent baldness which requires that he wear a plastic skullcap at night. It gives him the look of something out of Gilbert & Sullivan. I tried to turn my mind to such practical matters as the opening song for Act Two, for which I had a few lines on the pad I keep by the bed. But what I thought of was the way she had kicked off her shoes—like a horse kicking over the traces—and the number of times, and in how many places, she had done that before. Wide awake, not dreaming, mind you, I sat up in bed and drummed my fists on the wall until I saw Mac, like a corpse wearing a mud pack, rise up from his bed. I waited for him to bellow, "Christamighty, man!" but he didn't. Not a peep.

"Woman!" I said, I mean I almost shouted, and I thought I could see her, with that sea of kelp behind her, and when the dark spoke to me with her voice I put my tongue to my lips and realized they were sore.

If I'd known what the day was going to be like I'd not have got up.

Mac was up first. I found him in the bathroom squeezing blackheads and experimenting with an oil for people who want a tan but who can't stand the sun. You put this one on your skin with a little roller the way they now paint plaster in your apartment. It goes without saying how it looked on Mac.

"Why don't you just face it?" I said.

He put the tube down, exclaimed, *"Why don't we face it*! Christamighty, it's great! You know what I mean?"

When he sees a song hit in every remark, the die is cast—if you know what *I* mean. Eyes lidded, his pitted face shiny with love, he crooned:

"Why don't we just face it?"

"That's nice," I said. "What a pity that a song called "How Deep Is the Ocean?" has the same tune."

"That come out before my time," said Mac, injured.

"I know," I said, "both you and Bridey Murphy."

Repartee is not his great forte, so he said, "I told the chick I'd meet her down there at twelve," then he plugged in his razor so he wouldn't hear what I said. I didn't say it. I don't suppose I cared. I can't both love and bite the hand that feeds me, so I went out to the kitchen and poured some juice. I had to force it down. I wasn't sick. I just couldn't eat. In high school I fell in love with a girl who cost me my letter in basketball and tennis. I lost so much weight and got so weak I had to quit the team. She wore blue tennis sneakers on her long flat feet and carried a pencil box in a matching color, and either one of those objects will upset me to this day.

"I also told her," Mac said, "we'd have some friends around to meet her. You know what I mean?"

"You mean Hoppy and the boys?"

That was what he meant. Hoppy is a gent who entertains himself with the flotsam of show biz. He specializes, so to speak, in the boys who want just one more chance. By an odd sort of coincidence they are all red-lipped boys who impersonate girls. If you want to know what *else* Hoppy has, it's a controlling interest in the night-club circuit.

"If she's gonna make time," said Mac, "she's gotta make it with Hoppy." I didn't deny it, and he added, "I gave him a call. He said he'd bring the boys over."

I walked through the house to the phone I had used, put my juice on the floor, dialed the number. She answered.

"It's me," I said.

"Oh—" That was all.

"I hope I didn't catch you burping one of them," I said.

"There's always something."

"Are your lips as sore as mine?"

"Put baby oil on them," she said. Very matter-of-factly. Your Friendly Druggist giving you free advice. I had felt reasonably well. Suddenly I felt damp all over and weak. I took a grip on myself, said:

"You said to call—"

"I get one night off a week," she replied, "and that was last night."

"Look, Greek—" I began.

"I've had a hard life," I heard her say, as if she had turned to speak over her shoulder, "and I've come to realize you can't ignore the basic things."

"Right," I said, hardly caring what I said. "You are one of mine."

I think that stumped her. It did wonders for me. That feeling at the pit of my stomach that wouldn't go one way or the other, once I got that said it came right up.

"She's gone from twelve to one-thirty."

"Who is?"

"Mrs. Mattson."

"Where will you be?"

"I must stay here."

I paused a moment, as if before leaping, then I said: "I'll be there."

"Leave your car in the road," she said. "I'll be watching." Then she hung up.

I was still sitting there, my glass of juice on the floor, when Mac came along.

"You don't have to sneak off to do it, man. You know what I mean?"

"I got an appointment at twelve," I said, "so I'll run you down to the beach a little early."

"That chick's got to get clearance from me," he said. "You bring her around."

Just the idea made me weak again. Mac was a clown, a real slob, but if he happened to be part of her development—if she wanted to make him a gift of life?

"You don't look *good*, man," he said. "What kinda chick you call that?"

I left him there and went out on the sun deck over the garage. If you live in a world of clichés, as I do, some of them of the type you coined yourself, you may not realize how powerful they can be. Farther down the canyon, in one of those Good Places you see in *House Pitiful* every month, with a tile swimming pool the shape of a kidney, two or three chicks were spread out like towels drying in the sun. One had a coolie hat over her face, one lay on her tummy rather than her back, but either way fairly similar merchandise. They had a portable radio on a beach chair, and the boys were doing "On the Street Where You Live," the lyrics drifting up the canyon to my roof. You won't believe it, but I had to turn around and go in. That street where *she* lived, over off Kentwood, was just two or three canyons away, and I could see that drive, the flower bed on the turn, the gate opening into the court, and coming toward me on the lawn that goddess with the child on her hip.

The effect on me was about the same as the feeling I have about "The Song of the Lark," the painting that is, I forget who by, but a copy of it dominated my boyhood. That girl, too, with the scythe in her hand, had about her a simple womanly beauty that moved my nine-year-old heart to do strange things. The *song* of the lark, in a crazy way, not being there in the picture at all, was perhaps as close as we come to portraying the sentiments of love. You can see the effect well enough, but not the stimulus. Why a street no different from ten thousand others, on which I had been just once in my life, should almost make me weak to think about it, is both gruesome and marvelous—depending on your point of view. I was too ashamed to stay out there on the roof and face up to it. I went back to the kitchen and ate some cottage cheese, the way you would force down damp surgical dressing, then I remembered to shave, take a shower, and brush my teeth. My lower lip was so sore that it had cracked. We didn't have any baby oil around the place, but I found some rancid olive oil, left by the last tenant, and applied a little of that. I killed some more time packing the car with our usual beach paraphernalia, then went in and told Mac to snap it up. He did. It's one of the few advantages that come from worrying him.

A good half-hour earlier than he intended, I drove him down Sunset to the beach, where layer after layer of cotton-heavy fog was blowing in. Not more than two or three beach umbrellas had been put up. Really bleak;

one of those melancholy ruins you see so often in modern painting, dappled with bottles, cans, strips of newspaper, and a body or two. Mac was just too numb to complain about it. Real emotion leaves him speechless—I mean even *more* speechless—and we unloaded the car and pitched the camp without a word. As an extra piece of dog he had decided to wear a black velvet sports shirt, with nautical buttons, and his hairy white legs were streaked with this liquid tan. He was also chewing a wad of chlorophyll gum. I left him there with a strong impulse to kick a little of the sand on him, the way a cat puts something unpleasant out of sight.

It left me with half an hour to kill, so I drove around for ten minutes, going past the corner where I had picked her up. I went past the movie where she had stood for a moment out in front. I didn't remember until too late that I might have driven down to Malibu and looked at the place where we had spent part of the night. Finally I drove up the street where she lived, and up near the top, where the altitude got me, she suddenly drove by me with this station wagon full of kids. She was at the wheel, over on my side, and looked just great. A rather haggard, semipreserved female whom I took to be Mrs. Mattson sat on her right, a cigarette between her lips. She didn't look at all like a woman who would have

so many kids. But the turn today, I suppose, is to *have*
them, painless, painful, or what have you, then let someone else *raise* them till you can ship them off to school.

I parked in the road, as she had told me, then I killed
a quarter-hour by just walking around, peering over the
wall at the assorted dream houses and their swimming
pools. They all seemed to have a dog that would bark,
shared a Japanese gardener with their neighbor, and had
a sprinkling system to water their odorless flowers. If
looks mean anything, and they do, you can't beat such
looks. I'm the biggest fool in the world for pathos, and
you can't beat the pathos of a beautiful world in which
nobody, and I mean nobody, knows how to live. That
fact often makes me a little bitter, since I have to include
myself, but having lived in one way or another for a day
I was tolerant. I felt a tender pity for these ghosts, most
of them decent sorts of human beings, who had everything but a man or a woman to make their heads spin,
who had it all, lock, stock, and barrel. And it crossed my
mind at that moment that this was why they had settled
for these things. The man or woman being lacking, what
else was there? Houses and swimming pools.

I didn't mean a dream girl, or even my girl, but the
woman who in walking across a lawn makes your mouth
go dry with the sense of a fatal rendezvous. What that

spider probably feels, I suppose, when he meets the lady who dines on him. What a woman feels when she knows that the man lying there with her may give her a baby, and the man that he may soon have a sore on his lip. Well, let him, she says, and it is the *let him* that has gone out of it. Now it didn't make me bitter. I just felt sorry as hell for all of them.

I killed another twenty minutes brushing out the car, where I found a mother-of-pearl compact, a leather-covered lighter, and two prophylactics, unused. Signs of the times, that is. Mine and yours. That brought me to twelve, so I walked up the drive to the gate, where the colored maid had one of the little ones out in a pram.

"You the one for Eva?" she asked, and I said I was. I watched her face to see if that amused her, but she was a woman long accustomed to it. All Evas in general, that is, and the men who showed up for them.

I asked her how many kids there were and she said *five*, just the word five, but in such a way that she had the whole picture summed up in it. She rolled her eyes from the child in the pram to take in the house, the lot, and the sky. "She has 'em, we take care of 'em," she said, but she did not laugh.

Along the front of the house there were klieg lights of

the sort they have out in front of movie houses or sign-
boards they want lit up at night. She saw me looking at
them and said, "Mrs. Mattson scared to death of kid-
nappers. Eva tell you not to prowl around at night?"

I shook my head. No, Eva had not told me anything
like that. It might be that a middle-aging man might
think twice—while he could—before being shot down
in the driveway as a kidnapper. I wandered back down
the drive to my car and sat in the seat, for another twenty
minutes, till the station wagon came up behind me and
honked. The Greek was in it alone. She put her head out
to say, "You better hurry up, I've only got about half an
hour," without a word about the fact that I'd just waited
longer than that. I followed her car up the drive, then
followed her across the lawn to the door at the side,
which opened directly into her room. It looked like a
student's room, with a case of books, a desk with a
portable typewriter on it, a record player in one corner,
with a pile of sheet music on the floor. On her desk was
the picture of a young man in his cap and gown, confi-
dently smiling, and turning to see what it was I saw she
said: "My brother." That was all.

I waited while she slipped off what she had on and
slipped into a white dress, a uniform, then she said,

"Come—" and I followed her down one of the halls. We passed several children-littered rooms to the kitchen, where a frozen turkey thawed in the sink and the morning dishes were stacked to one side, waiting to be washed.

"I got behind," she said; "you're always behind," and put a saucepan on the stove, over a low fire, added a cup of water, and put the baby's bottle in it. From the icebox she took a carton of yogurt, from the shelf over the sink a can of fruit salad, stirred the fruit and the yogurt together, spooned out two helpings, and passed one of them to me. "You probably didn't have your lunch either," she said, and began to eat. I watched her eat, then she left the kitchen to return in a moment with the little one, soaking in his diaper. She placed him on the changing rack, slipped the diaper off, wiped him with a tissue, powdered him from a can, then folded him like a chop into a clean diaper. She went off with him, then came back and finished her lunch. I had not eaten a bite of mine and she said, "You *must* eat it. You need it," and put her own spoon into my bowl, fed it to me. I took a mouthful, but could hardly swallow. "This is not the time for your hurt feelings," she said. "*Eat.*"

"Along with my feelings," I said, "I can't stand canned fruit salad."

"Oh!" she said. "I'm sorry." She was.

"I don't mean to complain," I said. "This is California. You can't have everything."

She left the room and returned with the child, holding him in her arm so she could bottle feed him. He went for the bottle, but one waving hand found the opening to her dress, hooked on to her bra strap.

"If you knew me, I don't think you'd like me," she said. She did not raise her eyes to look at me.

"Maybe *he* wouldn't either," I said, and watched her slip his hand from inside of her dress. "I'm like him. I'm not so sure that it matters." She raised her eyes, and I added, "Not at this stage."

I held her gaze, she held mine, and I walked around the table, tipped back her head, and she repeated no, no, no, no, no—up to the moment I took her breath, nothing more, from her lips. She turned and went off with the child again, and from the room down the hall she said:

"You probably don't want children, do you—at your age?"

It was not something I had given any thought. I saw now that I wanted a child, but not if I thought he would deprive me of his mother. The lover, too, is a child. But the child-lover had the advantages.

"You better go now," she said. "She'll be back any minute."

I just stood there for a moment, doing nothing, then I left. I went down the hall but made a wrong turn into a bathroom, where diapers were drying, and several large plastic fish, with an assortment of boats, floated in the tub. I backed out and found my way to her room, out the door, and almost ran across the yard. The latent kidnapper in every man's conscience, I suppose. The inside of the car had got hot with the top up, and while I was trying to get it down, a cab, with Mrs. Mattson in it, came up the road and made the turn. A minute or two later, with the colored maid in it, it came back down. I drove back to Sunset, then west to the sea where the morning fog had lifted, the beach was crowded, and I had to hunt around for a place to park. I found Mac and his chick under the umbrella, tête-à-tête. They were playing through a pile of Mac's old records and drinking beer out of pint-size cans.

"It's a great day, man!" Mac yelled, and he looked pretty good. Either she had got him down into the water or dipped a rag in it and wiped off his streaky sun tan. He had a flush of color in his face, and the crucifix he wore looked like a war medal. Billie gave me her hand and a nice intimate sort of squeeze.

"How'd every little thing go, man?" asked Mac, and I rolled my eyes to indicate that it had gone splendid. "You gotta watch these chicks, man. They get emotional. You know what I mean?"

Christ knows why, but I suddenly sang:

> "A cannibelle's affection is a dangerous thing.
> She prefers the knuckle to the wedding ring.
> The banquet of love
> Is the one she cooks
> Without the aid of how-to-do-it books."

There was a silence. It lasted for some time, then Mac said:

"Man, how you fit that into the Mexican picture?"

"I'm working on it," I said. And sure enough, I was.

We ran up toward Santa Barbara for dinner, looking every inch the sort of people who are living the life that has escaped everybody else. The chick in between us— there is something touching about the single chick between the two wolves—and I could see the passing glances calculate which one of us boys was her own true love. What I mean to say is, we gave everybody his money's worth.

We had charcoal-broiled steaks at one of these clubs with the slanting windows, seeing-eye doors, and the glimmer of candles in the eyes of women fifty-five and up. The nicest people in the world, by their own standards, having eaten their farrow, buried their husbands, and now finally deserving a bit of the finer things in life. A little woman with the face of the smiling Christ and arms like the bags of shot they hang on ash trays, couldn't take her watering eyes off Billie's face. Two *men*. On the coast of California in a place called Mambo with *two* men.

The Mambo Ensemble came on about ten and consisted of four Fifty-second Street holdouts, one of whom Mac knew personally. A torch-type singer with that rocky hip tic that is considered to be sexy sang two Mexican songs for "ee-frr-poddys leesnink pleshr," as she said. Before she finished I had to revise my usual misconceptions of the public, and see a great future for Miss Harcum singing "What Next?" I didn't have long to wait. Mac had got up, I thought to make a trip to the men's room, but he walked up front and spoke to this bass fiddle player. By this fellow's standards, Mac was tremendous, being a man who wrote songs they actually paid for, and the effect on this group was magic. They all came to life. Even this torch singer until she heard that Mac had brought along his own little "towtch

singah." He came back to our table for Billie, then led
her up front, beside the piano, and by this time the excitement in this place was almost real. Right before
their eyes a star, caesarean, was being born. All of those
women who had known we must be *some*one were almost
out of their minds to see that they had been right. Mac
himself sat at the piano, turning on the stool so he could
beam at Miss Harcum, and there's no cliché in the world
to equal the guy who steps from the crowd, sits down at
the piano, and begins to play.

Her pretty little duckies pulsing in the spotlight, Billie
asked them all "What Next?" her voice a little shaky,
and even before she had given them the answer I knew
this was it. A talk piece, in the tradition of the "Two
Black Crows," the piano supporting the swimmer like a
pair of big loving hands. We had a new song, a new star,
a new hit.

Mac would have banged the piano all night—he can
time an entrance but not an exit—so I had to come forward and remind him that we had to run to make a TV
date. The fact that Mac could forget something like that
pleased everybody almost silly, being so much like what
Reader's Digest says show people are really like. The
management wouldn't think of our paying the check,

gave Billie the floral offering they had in the lobby, and turned the spotlights on our car when we left.

We had this wind in our sails going back, a sea with the moonlight painted on it, and in fifty-five minutes we were going up the canyon, where we could see our mansion was full of lights.

"What the hell's this?" I said, parking in the drive.

"Guess Hoppy an' the boys are here," said Mac. "I told 'em if we weren't back yet to make themselves at home."

They had come up in Hoppy's new Lincoln Continental. Nine of them. The Continental, as you may have read, is that conservative sort of car that so clearly reflects your quiet good taste. They'd left the radio on and it was playing rock 'n roll.

All the lights in the place were on, but when we came in, the crowd was up front, the rugs rolled back, and they were rehearsing a little show. As a rule Hoppy's parties are stag, if that's the word for it, but this performance included a pair of chicks. One about forty-five, I would say, an imported hand-rubbed-calf sort of item, very cool, with a long cigarette holder and calf-length pants. A chaperone, that is, for the little full halter on the sofa beside her, *café au lait*, with the emphasis on the lay.

They spoke only French. So "fery lil inklish to be shamt."

It's wonderful to see how one chick's mind begins to triumph over another chick's matter—both of them, of course, starting from scratch. Billie Harcum took one cool glance at the halter and transformed herself into Katharine Hepburn. All Bridle & Bit, suh, of the Hound and Horn class.

When Mac introduced her to Hoppy she gave him a nod, her pretty hands tightly clasped, the pleats in her upper lip very prominent. Hoppy is a man about my own age, one of those contemporaries you hate to meet, since you have to face it, the way he does, with a smile. The first four or five times we met I was absolutely certain I had met him before, knew him well, in fact, but the man he turns out to resemble is himself. Head bald, body hairy, a look that is both penetrating and friendly, and finds you smiling with him at yourself. What I dislike about him most is that I can't resist liking him. He's got money, he buys and sells people, but he does it with so much infectious good humor that you don't mind it at all when you see your own head on the block. He bought Mac at a bargain, and sold him at a nice markup. That deal included me, so I've always resented it. But he had

Miss Harcum sized up so well that her little cool act actually pleased him, like the mother of a brat who knows there's money in the nasty type.

"Ah, the poet," he said, taking my hand, "if you just had someone to write the music."

"Wait'll you hear it," bellowed Mac. "Man, it's great."

"Miss Harcum just stampeded the Mambo," I said, and about five of them hollered:

"Where's the Mambo?" In this racket any place that *might* stampede is the Great Good Place.

"Just a smart little club up the coast," I said, "near Santa Barbara."

Besides the birds of prey on the sofa, Hoppy had a crew *aus* Las Vegas, where one of the smaller clubs had just closed. Three tall boys, of the boat-crew type that came in, I'd say, with the Ivy League concept, all of them nervously langorous and sloppy in something from Italy. Young enough to be boys, old enough to be dissipated. *They* were the talents, but each of these boys had his own man Friday, a slice of the same cheesecake, the song-and-dance boys you see around the piano in the bars. Modified duck's ass hairdos, teeth that need repairing, and the sunny smile of hand-carved soap favors.

These boys once kept Sir Gawain's armor polished, reported on dragons, delivered notes to wooded castles, and picked their man up when he took a prat fall from his horse. Now all they polish is his apple. Their big job is to applaud.

"You got a show on your hands?" I said to Hoppy, and took a quick smiling glance at the *talent. One* of the boys on the sofa sprang to life. Not all of them, mind you, just one, and the way this pecking order operates, in this hen yard of egos, is a wonderful thing to behold. The one who *has* a talent, or a *job,* bides his time on the sofa in a casual manner while the washed-up side-kick goes through his washed-up little act. A big, good-looking, almost healthy youngster led off. Black hair, sparkling eyes, with a certain Harold Teen sort of touch in his manner, he sang a sad little ballad about young love, then wet his lips, leered and said:

"*Do* the Duke an' the Duchess?"

You get the effect? He did. While he hoped you were laughing he leaped from the piano, yanked an accordion out of its case, and gave us the "Lay of Capri," the screaming lyrics all by himself. Between choruses, in his stocking feet, he did an original soft-shoeless number, the sort of thing we owe to Martha Graham and the time on our hands at night. His man Friday slipped in at that point with his clarinet, a Ted Lewis-type top hat, and acting like Fred Astaire he sounded like Benny Goodman, and looked like himself. He followed that with a guitar, collapsing on the floor to sing an Afrikander ballad and a prison song, then leaped up, sobered, to impersonate Maurice Chevalier. Like Smirnoff's vodka, it fairly took your breath away. His man Friday screamed and ran around the room with his hat extended, scratching himself like a monkey, and in the friendliest manner possible Hoppy said:

"When he learns about the musical saw, he'll have an act."

But he wouldn't. Not in Hoppy's night-club circuit.

I went to get myself a stiff one at that point, so I missed the one who played like Fats Waller, but the applause came in pretty well through the heating system. When I got back, the talented number, this loose rubbery boy with the dissolute smile, was giving his impersonation of Marlene Dietrich in Las Vegas. He wore a lamp shade, and had pulled his pants halfway up his thighs. He had the sort of talent, the uncoached, untutored natural talent all Americans *love*, beginning with his mother who was the first to say that he did what he did without a single little lesson. He did, all right. And that was how it looked. Even Mac in this particular case had a look of cynical pity on his face, and later he would tell me what a goddam shame such a waste of talent was. The kid sensed that, so we couldn't shut him up. He dug around in his old bag of parlor tricks for one that might work. His man Friday could neither shut him up nor help him—you little *pimp,* he yelled at him, you're just jealous—then he saved us all a nasty scene by gulping down his drink and passing out. We laid him out on the floor where there was a cool offshore breeze. He had a beardless teen-ager's face, pimpled at the hairline and around the lips, and with his hands finally quiet you could see that he'd chewed his nails to the quick. The second knuckle on his right hand was actually raw. Not having been able to eat for days, that sort of cannibalism interested me.

To pick the party up a little Hoppy said:

"Should we have the pee-ass de resistance now?"

And Mac bellowed, "Let's have it now," being full of heart but five days without sex.

"Den I moos chanche—" said the little girl in the halter, by which she meant a slight rearrangement, since there was little she had on that would come off. I led her back to an empty room, where she could *chanche,* and she asked me, "Pliss, for a gol glas wadr. No boooos. Jus wadr an lil ize."

I got her the glass of water, full of ice cubes, then I stepped out on the roof over the garage. The glittering jewel box along the coast was all lit up. Lights were on around the pool a little lower in the canyon, the water so clear and smooth I could see the pattern of the tiles at the bottom of it. There was no music, but having stood there for a moment in the morning I seemed to hear the words of that song about the street where she lived. It made me, as it had at the time, just a bit weak. I stepped into my bedroom and stretched out on the bed until it passed. My room was dark, but the door to the bathroom was open, and this little girl with her glass of ice water stood facing the mirror. I watched her empty the water into the sink, but retain the ice. She put the loose cubes in a face towel, whacked them on the edge of the sink until she had crushed them, then took the crushed ice, a handful of it, and slipped it into the cups of her halter. All the ice she had; then she cupped it to her breasts. I saw her face reflected in the mirror, the eyes closed in a grimace of pain, the teeth clamped down on her lower lip till it turned white. She stood there till the ice had produced a numbness and the pain had passed. Then she took off the halter, examined her breasts as though they were tires that had been recapped, felt the firmness of the flesh, and applied a yellow cream that she took from a jar. She turned off the light switch, then stood there, turning from left to right, seeing in the mirror how her breasts glowed in the dark. Still in the dark, her fingers glowing, she painted her lips and eyes with the luminous salve, daubed a bit on her navel, then left the room.

I didn't see the performance. From the way they applauded, it must have been good. I fell asleep with my clothes on, shoes and all, my stiff drink on the floor beside me, and I slept until the ringing of the telephone woke me up.

"Hello?" I said.

It was the Greek. I was too astonished to believe it.

"Did I get you up?"

"I'm getting up."

"I got the night off," she said.

"Night? When?"

"Nine, but I have to be back at twelve."

"Where?"

"Here. Come at nine," she said.

"I'll be there," I replied, and heard her hang up. Mac had come to the door to see who the hell would call at

111

that time in the morning. His plastic hat was still on his head. He looked like a freak. I put the receiver on the hook, said:

"I take it everything went all right?"

"Man, she was terrific."

"With or without the lights?" I said.

"Not her, man!" he said. "I mean the chick. Hoppy says she's got a great future."

"Hmmmm," I said, and wondered what she would think of her future in his skullcap.

"He says she's great. He took her home personally in his car."

Was I saying—until I met her—that the pitch of this age is phony? It's phony as hell, but as Mac once said, "What the hell, man. What else is there?" The phony *is;* I mean it's here and now, and all that once was or is yet to be *isn't.* You've got to take what's phony, if it's all you've got, and make it real.

"You hear me, man?" said Mac. "Hoppy says she's great."

"I heard you," I said, then got out of bed and went into the kitchen, where I peeled a banana, since you have to eat to live, whether its phony or not. Mac slipped some ice cubes into the lining of his skullcap and went back to bed.

IV

We didn't go to the beach. We stayed in bed most of the day. Mac called Billie Harcum to say that the pressure of work would keep him at home during the day, but we would pick her up for a drink about six o'clock. In the afternoon I lay out on the roof drinking tomato juice. As Mac said, "You got to eat, man. It's good for the *team.*"

I suppose Mac lives, if that's the word, in the sand-lot world of Toots Shor, where every man has his own set of goal posts and his own team. I was on Mac's team, he was on mine, and we were going to face the music to-gehhh-thurrr.

He paced up and down the porch in a terry cloth bathrobe once given to him by a Golden Gloves boxer, the words "ST. DAVID'S BOYS" stitched across the back. He's just pitiful when he gets upset and man to man. In the army you could put a helmet on him, stick him in the turret with some guns, then let him just shoot hell out of everything in sight. The song-and-dance business lacks that sort of fire power. I've often wondered what I would do if Mac cracked up—do with him, that is—since most people would hardly notice the difference. He has about all the symptoms. He simply doesn't go to bed with them. What he was suffering from now was the trouble he could feel at headquarters—me, that is—and he can't stand trouble like that. So long as I have things under control, so does he. About a quarter to four he blurted it out:

"Man, what's this chick want?"

"Me," I said. "I'm part of her development."

"You're just lettin' this woman use you, man. You can't let a woman use you—"

"You can't?" said I. I had often said as much. "She can," I said, "bless her, and she does."

That really scared the hell out of him, as well it might. Here I was out of my mind with a chick he had never set eyes on.

"You gotta snap out of it, man," he barked. "We got this show. We got this—"

"Mac—" I said, soberly, "how long will it take you to pack?"

"Look—" he said.

"We're going to Mexico," I said, "to work. I want to get the feel of the place, the people."

"Great!" he bellowed. "Christ, man, that's great."

"You want to take that little chick along?" I said.

"Chick?" He just eyed me.

"I'll be taking mine along," I said, "and you might feel left out."

For two, three minutes, which can be a long time, he just stood there. The disadvantage of an ice pack is what it does to promote what is seldom referred to as pallor. I was the one who was weak, but he looked it.

"Look—" he peeped.

"You better give her some time to think it over," I said, "just so she'll know how thoughtful you are. You might just throw in, casually you know, that we'll be picking up the cast as we go along. We can't help but be a little influenced by the people we have handy."

"Look—" he said once more, but not like he meant it.

"You better go call her," I said, "since we'll be leaving in the morning. It's a long drive. We'll need about a week to get the feel of the place."

He said, "What place?"

"Acapulco," I replied. That was one place she had heard of.

115

He started off, then he turned and said, "You sure?"

"About what?"

"This chick of yours?"

I was not.

"Don't worry," I said, "she'll see that it's part of her development."

He went and put through a call, then he came back and said, "I told her to take a cab and come right over. I told her we had an important decision to make." I knew that wasn't all he told her, and he added, "Man, suppose *we* put it to her. She likes to hear you talk. It's quite a proposition. You know what I mean?"

I put on a lounging outfit Mac once gave me that I've never known what the hell to do with, but I could see it was just the thing for a quiet little talk. When her cab pulled up in the drive I went in and sat at the piano, put a score on the rack, and a pencil over one ear. When Mac brought her in I was bent over the score, frowning. They waited. I let them wait. I scribbled down a few words, then I turned and said:

"Billie, the heat is on. We got to do a little location work in Mexico, and if you could spare a couple weeks at this time—we need someone along to track the new stuff—and it might be the sort of thing you would find interesting. We tend to write the stuff for a certain performer, and—"

"Uhl, honey, if ah could be of any help—"

"Think you might," I said, "and if Mac thinks so—"

"She's great, man!" barked Mac. She gave him her hand, and while she gazed into his eyes, he gazed into hers.

"Break it up, kiddies," I said, "we leave in the morning, so you probably have a few little things to do."

"Uhl, honey—not tomorra mornin'?"

"At about ten A.M.," I said, picking up my pencil, the score, and brought the scene to a close on just the right pitch. "You'll need something to show you were born," I said, "and we'll have to pick you up a smallpox vaccination. Acapulco, as you know, is not a pasteurized sort of place."

About fifteen minutes later they went off together in the cab she had come up in, and I made some black coffee, opened some sardines, and actually finished them off. I would need what strength I could muster when I faced the Greek.

With past experience to guide me I put on some comfortable slacks, a light nylon sweater, some canvas sneakers, and at half-past eight drove over and parked on the street where she lived. Sitting there in the car the scene I had in mind arranged itself. "Any place in particular?" I would say, and she would reply.

"Any place."

Then we would go back to that place in Malibu where she would kick off her shoes as she entered the door. I would have made the trip, I think, just for that. And then, after first things first, we would talk, in the vein of the previous occasion, and very casually I would pull Mexico out of my hat. I'd say just one week, rather than the two I had in mind, since she might find it hard to get two weeks off at this time of year. I would say, absolutely frankly, that I didn't really know what the hell I was doing, but I had to be with her if I was going to do *any*thing. Come what may. I had no idea what it might be. If *she* had one I would like to be part of it. All I hoped was that Mexico might fit in with her current development—but I'd use some other word.

At three minutes to nine I got out of the car and walked up the drive, through the gate, and just as I stepped off the asphalt onto the grass those damn lights came on. All five of them, going up like a wall right before me, and it turned that yard into something like a prison court. I froze stiff. I waited for that shot in the back of my head. The way you'll do, at such a crazy moment, I wondered if I'd hear the shot that would kill me or be dead before the sound waves got to my ears. But nothing happened. Not a thing. Just the click of the metal hoods on the lamps as the bulbs warmed up. On the white wall of the house I could see the flickering flight of some big moth. Nobody yelled, no alarms went off, so I went along the flagstone steps in the lawn to the door at the side, the one to her room. I gave it a very light tap, and she said, "Come in." I opened the door cautiously, peered in, and there she was in bed.

She had her head propped on some pillows, a book in one hand, a cigarette in the other, and after giving me a warm, superficial smile she returned to her gum.

"You sick?"

"Mr. Mattson called long-distance from New York but he missed Mrs. Mattson, so he has to call again. Somebody just has to be here to receive the call." She cracked the gum.

I suppose the two pillows behind her head made her hair stick up and look a little frowsy. She wore one of those sheer honeymoon gowns advertised for their transparent glamour, but it was in the wrong color, and somehow it wasn't her style. I was reminded again that no woman looks good sitting up in bed.

"Hmmmmm—" I said, stepping inside, and for the first time noticed the posters on the walls. Big prewar German travel posters. The ruins along the Rhine. Then I looked at the modern Rhine maiden in the bed. I hate parallels. But there it was.

"Come sit down," she said, and patted the bed.

"You had to go to bed," I said, "to answer the phone?"

"I am raising and feeding five children," she replied. "You know what that's like?"

"What you reading?" I said, to change the subject.

"Dostoevski." She actually was. "About the white nights of Russia," she added.

I tried to recall the white nights of Russia, but the dark night at Malibu intervened. In her ash tray was an apple core, just beginning to darken, a wad of pink gum, and half a dozen cigarette butts.

"There's another awful thing—" she began, then put down her book and sat up straight. A car was coming up the drive and the lights came through the windows, flashed on the walls.

"You've got to hide," she said, looking around, "somewhere."

"I've got to what?"

"She's going to come back here and look at the baby. She's going to ask me if her husband called."

I was sitting on the bed. I got up and tried to look under it. A camp locker and some soup cartons took all of the space.

"There's a closet—" she said, waving her arm behind her, and I walked to the corner and looked into the closet. It was packed with her clothes and had her shoes and a vacuum cleaner on the floor. There was no room to stand, anywhere, so I pulled out the vacuum cleaner, got in behind it, then crouched down on the floor. Just in time. I heard the door close at the front of the house. Two of the older kids came running through the house right to her room, ganged inside, and plopped down on the foot of her bed. They were all out of wind but dying to tell her about the movie they had just seen. She let them ramble till Mrs. Mattson came back, who asked them to please be quiet, then inquired about the call from New York. Eva told her that he would probably call again. Mrs. Mattson left the room and came back once more to speak to the children. The Greek yawned and said that she was all worn out.

"Who belongs to this?" asked one of the kids, and I

knew. It was my hat. I'd left it on the floor or the foot of the bed.

"My brother's," she replied. "Isn't it nice?"

I heard the girl try it on. "It's big for me," she said. "But I can wear it," said the Greek, and tried it on.

"Now you look like your boy friends," one said, but they left when she asked them to leave. She asked them to come back and close the door, and one of them did. I sat there on the floor, on the toes of some rubbers, my eyes on the crack of light beneath the door, listening to the bed the Greek was lying on creak and twang as she laughed. As I've told you several times, I'm forty-one. My hair is gray at the temples and there are slight pouches under my eyes. When she finally had the strength to open the door, and looked in and saw me, that set her off again. To keep from laughing hysterically she bit down on her arm. I saw the teeth marks on the flesh when I came out. I crawled out: sitting had made me stiff and there was no room in the place to stand upright. Out in the room I stayed on the floor beside her bed. It was three or four minutes before she got control of herself. That's just time enough, for a man of my age, to reconsider what had happened and reach the conclusion that the world's greatest jackass was himself.

In her fit of giggling she had stretched out face down on the bed, hugging her pillow, and the foot of her left leg dangled near my face. The polish on the nails had been cracked for some time. The heel was dirty. It was not a pretty foot, nor a pretty ankle, nor was it attached to a pretty leg. The girl was tremendous as a piece, but not in the parts. There were several swollen mosquito bites on her arms. Before she stopped wheezing I had made something like peace with my situation, had brushed the lint off my knees, found and put on my hat. But I had to wait till the house was quiet before I could leave. Now that the lady was home I might really get that shot in the back.

She was still sprawled on her face when she said:

"Didn't I tell you you wouldn't like me?"

"You did," I said, "and you were right."

"Does it matter—now?"

I was slow to answer. I don't know why. It mattered to beat hell, right at the moment, but I suppose I wanted to believe in the past. She rolled on the bed to look at my face, her own wet with tears of laughter, and that piece of pink chewing gum at the front of her mouth. She reached for the hat I had put on, tossed it on the bed, and ran her hand through my hair.

"Let me tell you what I like, *first*," I said, "just in case I might forget it. You haven't lied to me. There has been no talk about love. You said that I aroused your desire, and I suppose I did. I said you were one of my basic needs, and you are. I think it's fairly unusual for a man and woman, more or less strangers, to lie so little to each other and still do so much."

She did not reply, and I went on. "As part of your development you should know what I had planned. I came here to sell you a bill of goods on Mexico. It's a wonderful place. We're doing a little musical on the subject, a sort of Love Among the Cannibals number, and it crossed my mind that the songs might be better if I knew a little cannibelle, personally. One like you. One I was really crazy to eat. I'd be wonderfully frank. I'd only lie to you on one small point. I'd tell you that a week would be long enough, but I'd kidnap you with two weeks in mind. As you know, two weeks can be a long time. If they were anything like the last thirty-six hours I wouldn't be around at all, at the finish, so one week would probably prove to be more than enough. That's what I would tell you—we would be lying, of course, on that bed in Malibu—and there's only one thing I like to do more than lie in bed with you and talk. We'd have done that, so the talking would be all right. Then I would mention, just in passing, that if Mexico sounded interesting to you, it just so happened that we had a vacant seat in the car. In case you'd like to come along you might meet me, say, about ten in the morning. To that you would reply, 'Any particular place?' and I would say, 'Make it the same place,' meaning that corner on the campus where I picked you up."

She pushed the pillow from under her head so that her eyes dropped down on a level with mine.

"When my friend Mac asked me if I was crazy enough to let a woman use me—you know what I replied? I said yes. Yes, if that woman was you. I want to be used. I mean I'd like to be used till I'm worn out. As for whether I like you, or you like me, it's something like the hand asking the body if it likes what it can't help reaching for. And I reach for you."

She closed her eyes, parted her lips, and I said, "But now I'm going to cut you, the way you've cut me. Just to see if you'll bleed. You seem to think that a lover is a bar-bell exerciser for your soul, a set of Indian clubs for your inner development. But you know what you are?" She waited. "You're a baby cannibelle. You like raw meat. You like to eat it alive. You have eaten my heart, the strings of my eyes, you have eaten my lights, my guts and my liver, and if you had a chance you would scoop out the hollow of my skull."

She did not deny it. Opening her eyes, her gaze on mine, she said, "And you?"

"I'm a cannibal too," I said, and reached for her hand, the arm with her teeth marks. "You see?" I said. "We are two cannibals," and I put my lips to the wound, bit her, and crooned:

> "A cannibelle's affection is a dangerous thing.
> She prefers the knuckle to the wedding ring.
> The banquet of love
> Is the one she cooks
> Without the aid of how-to-do-it books."

My words, if not my intentions, made love to her. Her hand was still in my hair, and it drew me toward her, down to her lips, her beautiful mouth, where the pink gum was stuck to the yellow tooth until I put it aside.

A police car made a tour of the place a little later and flashed its spotlight on the windows and around the yard. I don't think she heard it. Her breathing was deep and regular. I carried my shoes so I wouldn't make a racket in the gravel, and remembered too late that I'd

126

left my hat on the floor. I drove back to our mansion, where I found Mac, in the room with the mirrors, trying on the tropical touring clothes he had bought, English walking shorts, a pith helmet, and several pairs of sand boots.

"I take it the chick's in the bag?" I said.

He smiled. That inimitable full-of-heart, baby-face smile.

"We'll probably be alone," I said. "I figured the girls wouldn't take to each other."

He dropped his pants on the floor. Then he remembered what they cost him, picked them up.

"Man, you crazy?"

"Everything for the team!" I said.

He watched me cross the room to the hallway, where he suddenly remembered he had something to tell me.

"Man—" he said, "guess what, man." I didn't guess, so he added, "We still goin' to Acapulco?"

I nodded.

"Guess what, man. We got a free house. We got a villa, which is what they call it. Says there's fruit to beat hell just growin' all over. All you need to do is just lean out and pick it."

"Who says?"

"Guy who owns the villa. He's up here right now. Says we're welcome to it. Says bay is so close you can almost spit in it. How you like that, man?"

All I wanted to do, right at that point, was get away. Acapulco was away. It was also far away, and it was free. We could write off the chick as part of the production, but the studio's experience with song-writing teams ruled out villas, especially those in Acapulco, as part of the act.

"Ah'm sho yoh an' Miss Hah-cum will luv it," I said.

"What about another li'l chick?" said Mac. "What about a li'l Acapulco chick, f'rinstance?"

Just to keep him off the subject I said, "I told the Greek I'd let her know in the morning."

"*Who*—man?" he barked.

I didn't reply. He had heard me the first time, for he said, "The Greek? Christamighty man, whatta name." He shook his head, then said, "Too bad she's not goin' along."

V

At a quarter to ten we picked up Billie Harcum in a Bullock's Wilshire version of the *femme fatal*. Also five pieces of aluminum luggage, roughly the size of two steamer trunks, one of them so heavy Mac could hardly carry it to the car. You have to draw the line somewhere, so I said:

"Billie, dahlin'—there's a luggage limit at the border. Two bags per bag. Which two do you pick?"

About forty minutes later we had those five bags packed into two. I managed to get her to leave about forty pounds of toothpaste, cold cream, shampoo, and skin food. Somebody had told her there were no *white* women in Mexico.

Purely as a matter of sentiment I drove down Sunset to the UCLA campus, then across the campus to the corner where I had first picked her up. All I wanted to do, I suppose, was reassure myself. See with my own eyes the spot that marked the scene of the accident. You won't believe it when I tell you, but Mac saw her first. He simply said *Wow,* not particularly forceful, but the way it escapes you when you mean it. Up ahead, all alone on that corner, was my Greek. It looked to me like the purest coincidence. She had a sort of striped beach bag with her, nothing else, and I didn't even swing the car over toward her. I just made the stop I had to for the STOP sign, then we sat there and watched her walk around to my side. I think she saw that I couldn't speak, so she said:

"My mother is sick."

"*Who?*" I said, then, "She is? For how long?"

"She's going to be sick for just a week," she replied.

"A week," I repeated. So she had wangled a week. But nothing really registered until she said, "But if there isn't room?" and looked at the two beside me in the seat. That did it. I turned to Mac and said, "You kids mind moving into the rear?"

"Christ no!" barked Mac, meaning every word of it, and started to climb over the back before he remembered Billie. He slid back and let himself out the door, the normal way. But when Billie stepped out, I wasn't sure at all she would climb back in. But she had bought all that luggage, all those tropical rags, and she had probably told her friends what a dream she was living. So she decided to live it. The girls were never officially introduced. If you've ever noticed the way a big show dog will get into a car with a ficey small one, you've got the picture. It's not one to take at the start of a trip.

Somewhere along the freeway east of Palm Springs it occurred to me that in the past I had run off with books, rather than women, to Mexico. Books, that is, were my idea of self-development. One of the things I seemed to resent about the girl with her legs tanning in the seat beside me was that she preferred to take her life and literature raw. Having read me, mind and body, she would then move on to somebody else.

One of the books I took to Mexico had been on the bullfight, which I thought I had better read up on, but what I remembered was the author's advice to go to Spain. *Ronda.* They held bullfights in Ronda, but that was not it. Ronda was where you should go in case you *bolted* with someone. That word caught my eye at the time because I had wanted to bolt with someone, but hadn't. I was saving myself, at the time, for those marvelous girls that never turn up, most of them having bolted with somebody else or settled down with some books. Pride had kept me from asking a slant-eyed girl who worked the night shift at the local diner, and fear that she would turn me down kept me from asking the girl I was mad about. Pride and fear, that is, made me scrupulous. A young man with high principles, I bolted with myself. I had a fine time in Mexico, which I recommend to bolters who don't get to Ronda, but I did not see the country reserved for those who bolt with someone. I didn't cross that line. I turned back at that frontier.

When you hear people complain about customs regulations, passports, officials, and the rest of it, they are really telling you they don't want to leave the interior. They've come to a line, real and imaginary, they don't want to cross. When you bolt it helps to have one on the map, plainly visible. A threshhold. Like the door to that cabin in Malibu. When the Greek crossed that line she knew it, and kicked off her shoes. I like that. That's life as literature. You can have an affair in any old place, but in order to bolt with a woman you've got to cross a line, a frontier, in your interior. You've got to burn certain bridges that won't be there in case you come back.

In El Centro, where we stopped for coffee, Mac heard the gas attendant tell me that it was so-and-so many miles to the state line.

"State line, man?" he said. "We cross a *state* line?"

"It's not a line, Mac," I said, "it's a river."

But that didn't help. This line was not on the map. It was down in Mac's interior. He led me off to the men's room to tell me that if we *crossed* that line—the chicks had a case. A veteran of forty-three bombing missions, I'd never seen him so scared. I bought a comb from the comb dispenser and stood facing the mirror, combing my hair, while he made up his mind whether to cross that line or not.

"What's in it for me?" he asked.

"Ten to twenty years," I said, "or a photogenic Latin wedding."

Nothing amuses him so much as the idea of marriage, but he didn't laugh. When we came back to the lunchroom the girls were gone but their lipstick-stained cups were there, with five cigarette butts in Billie's saucer, one in the Greek's. You know that uneasy feeling you have when the women make peace? This pair of chicks who couldn't stand the sight of each other came up the stairs arm in arm, my big German police dog and Mac's little drugstore marble faun. They still hated each other, but they had established common ground. I've seen that happen time and again—the men go to the men's room and come back the same—but the women come back with all Gaul divided into two parts. Mac felt that worse than I did, since he relies on the women fighting. "Keeps their fire scattered, man," he says. "You know what I mean?"

But their fire was not scattered. "Man—" he began, but I replied:

"When they start like *that* you know how they end up?" He did, and smiled. I did too, but I didn't smile. It crossed my mind, watching the pair of them walk up, that there would be more than the usual hell to pay if my big police dog took a strong dislike to this marble faun. At that point part of Gaul would be divided into many parts. We gave them money to buy what they thought they would need, which is what women do when they face a decision: when they prepare to cross that interior line, I mean. My Greek spent twenty-eight fifty on herself, including a charge of thirty cents for me. What they call a chapstick. For lips that had got a bit chapped. Since her own were quite a bit that way, she figured mine were too.

We crossed the Colorado River a little after midnight,

a stream that Mac took a long careful look at, then we cruised along in the moonlight without the lights. The Greek picked up some music from south of the border on the radio. She curled up in the seat, her feet in my lap, a wad of Dentine gum in her mouth, a Hollywood Mexican-style bandanna wrapped around her head. The effect was that of a contraband bust wrapped for smuggling in assorted rags. Billie Harcum sat erect, her pony tail whipping the wind, the moonlight reflected in her Polaroid glasses, a film of cold cream shining like varnish on her lips. Mac held her hand, her box of Kleenex, and her Parliament cigarettes.

Over near Tucson I dozed off a little and almost missed a curve. The sway of the car rolled the Greek off the seat and woke up the pair asleep in the back. The car was headed east when it straightened out, and on the rim of the sky, like a crack in space, there was a luminous gap between the earth and a strip of cloud.

"A fie-ah?" cried Billie. "A foss fie-ah?"

"That's the dawn," I replied, "the crack of dawn."

"Ah sweah to God, Uhl, honey, ah thought the crack of dawn was a metaphoah!"

Far to the south we could see the lights of Nogales, where we planned to cross the border, and Mac relied

135

on the authorities to save him from himself. But they were very gracious. They made it inadvisable to observe the law. To have turned back would have been an insult to them and to Mexico. For a slight consideration we received our visas, the address of a man who would vaccinate the ladies, then we exchanged our dollars for pesos, and entered Mexico.

Book Two

I

Old lecher with a love on every wind, and you young ones too, running in pimpled packs after the teen-age bitch with her perfumed heat, and you, too, pretty matron, under the hair dryer, this is your book. The night is what you want, and you are waiting to hear *what next*. Love among us cannibals is not so bad we can ever get enough of it—unless, as sometimes happens, one of them turns up sick. Even a cannibal can lose his appetite. In the mountains near Guaymas an Indian woman sold Mac some pink bananas, with a sharp, wild flavor, along with cups of shaved ice sprinkled with syrup from Wildroot hair tonic bottles. That took care of me and Mac. That took care, I mean to say, of everything.

We ate the bananas, then sipped the ice the way you kiss the girls in the white-slave fiction, knowing we would soon come down with something as a keepsake.

And we did. Mac came down in Guaymas. Billie Harcum came down in Mazatlán. She had guessed it would happen, sooner or later, and had brought with her a book by Norman Vincent Peale on the 44 Practical Ways to Happier and Healthier Living. She read parts of it to Mac, so he was sick longer than usual.

I put off coming down until the Greek, who was sick in Tepic, was on her way up. That was in Guadalajara, where I had looked forward to a wonderful night. We had a suite with Simmons beds, single beds, one of them for each of us. During the long night the Greek rinsed the towels, emptied the pan in the shower drain, and lay beside me like a heater since the night was cool and I had come down with the chills. Everything I had bolted the day before, that night I lost. It occurred to me that nausea was just a way of bolting in reverse. It gives you time to taste, at length, all of the things you may have hastily swallowed. Since I had swallowed the Greek first, she came up last. She came up, that is, to where I could taste her—the lips, the yellow tooth, and the sharp tang of her sunburn—but I would have died rather than lose her, so she stuck in my throat. I couldn't get her to go up or down, and it gave me such a scare I grabbed hold of her.

"If you're as well as all of that—" she said, and pushed me away.

"I'm not," I replied, meaning as well as all that, then I blurted out, "but I don't think it matters!"

"If it doesn't," she said, "then what does?"

"Bolting with you," I said, and took a fresh grip on her. "Bolting with you is what matters."

She took the towel and wiped my face as if to see there what I meant. She saw it all right, then said:

"Is that *all* that matters?"

"No it's not *all*," I replied, and squeezed her so hard I was surprised at my own strength. "You don't live on what you eat, you live on what you keep down," I said. She wiped my face with the towel again, and said:

"You're getting well awfully fast," and I could see that I was.

Toward morning we had a gale, sheets of rain lashed the windows, and in the white flashes of theatrical lightning I could see her face with the marble smile on her lips. I wanted to wake her and tell her I would even settle for *that*. But I didn't, of course, since she would be the first to tell me that the smile would not be there in such a settlement. I could see her in that yard, the child straddling her hip, coming toward me with that smile on her lips, and I was strong enough to push that child out of the picture and take his place.

One of the risks you run when you bolt is that the woman you loved in the dark is there in the morning, as if you had forgotten to take her home. There she is. Like that girl in your arms when the music stops. The lump of the night you can take in one bite, the way a dog wolfs his food, but the lump of the day is what you have when you wake up.

I woke up feeling better, and there might have been a problem if the Greek had been there. A hotel lobby and a pair of lovers face the same impasse at ten in the morning. How to get through the day. How to get through the day without ruining the night. Few love affairs would fail to pan out if the night was as long as it is in the Arctic. What they fail to survive is the ten-hour day. With the light of day, as we say, the lying begins.

Our room had doors that opened on the mountains and a huge photo mural of the bay of Acapulco. The mural almost fooled me. The green mirror of the sea in the curve of the bay. All around it the gleaming air-conditioned pleasure palaces. On the white sand of the beach what you would find on beaches everywhere. Shells, oil smears, prophylactics, and human flesh served up according to taste. Not in the picture were the oily-skinned boys with the lips and eyes of fish out of water, their mouths full of evil and the calypso chatter of gold teeth. I lay there gazing at it, through the rain-scoured light, until Mac came in and told me that the girls had gone shopping. It made me smile. Our chicks were smart. They knew what the problem was. If they could get through the day, it would be up to us boys to get through the night.

Any way you cut it, day or night, I was the one who got the most for my money, since the price of the clothes they bought was the same but it took twice the material to cover my girl. They both put on their new rags, with the Hollywood labels, and we finally got away about four o'clock—we got away, I mean, after passing out pesos like soap coupons. We took along enough hot tea, toast, and Kaopectate to make the next stop. That night we had to make one hotel room do—I mean the girls had to make it do, since there was just one bed, and they slept in it. The way they went about it, the way they *didn't*, indicated that Mac had little cause for worry. We men, that is. The chicks were cooling off. Miss Harcum made

143

it clear that even a double bed was hardly big enough for my police dog, and my police dog made it more than clear she was right. To see the girls bristling did Mac more good than the medicine. He lay out on the sofa and I sat out on the balcony. Right below me a young man strummed his guitar, serenading a *muchacha* whose lips, he said, were like rose petals, and whose dark eyes were bottomless as forest pools. That's what he told her. In between her numbers he serenaded me, and in the hope that the night would result in something he doffed his sombrero and inquired if the ladies had any requests. The ladies were asleep, but I requested "What Next?" He hadn't heard of that, so I put in a plug for Macgregor & Horter, tipping him off that the song was now sweeping the States. In return he sang me "Three Coins in the Fountain," then reported that los Yanquis de Nueva York had clubbed los Gatos Rojos de Boston by a score of 11 to 3. We were doing so well, and the future looked so bright, that he wished me health, I wished him likewise, and in the dawn light I watched two little Indians take the hubcaps off our car, then sit on the fenders waiting for us. Across from us was a church, moist as a cave, and when the doors swung open I could hear the children, somewhere at the front, chanting together like caged birds. While I bargained with the boys about the hubcaps three or four others washed and polished the car, including in their fee, as one of them pointed out, the return of the hubcaps to the wheels. When we got in and moved on they ran along beside us, like a pack of hounds, pointing out the sights, the holes in the road, and finally the highway that led wherever we wanted to go. That was still Acapulco, where we had a house on the Calle de Juarez, overlooking the sea, unless there had been a revolution or an earthquake and the name or the location of the street had changed. Mac's studio friend had supplied him with a map, which we stopped in Chilpancingo to look at, showing the curve of the bay and the beautiful location of his house. Besides the beautiful location, the house was being modernized. A Señor Eroza, caretaker, along with his wife, would be at our service. No key was necessary. We would find him on the grounds.

Out of Chilpancingo we went over the mountains and the hot dry wind was suddenly moist. The road curved along a stream of fast water, running almost white in the rapids, holding the light from the sky long after the canyon was dark. Now and then we caught a whiff of the tropical sea. We picked up Acapulco on the radio, a big, good-neighborly sort of band, sounding like Glenn Miller, playing the sort of jazz that would please the tourist crowd. Myself, Mac, and the girls we had along with us, that is. I turned up the volume, and my Greek, who had been curled up in her corner, rocked herself over and lay with her head in my lap. The night air got so moist we seemed to be floating, the breeze almost lapped on the car, and we came out on the rise, as if we had surfaced, with a view of the sea. The bay of Acapulco, trimmed with lights, after the long dark drive through the mountains, was like the jewel box of the coast seen through that window where I first saw the Greek. Anything that is so right, that seems perfect, is followed by a state of apprehension, which reminds you how imperfect perfection really is. Coasting down the rise into the lights I said:

"Any particular place?"

And she replied, "Any place."

So we had done it again, and I said:

"Greek, close your eyes," and she closed them. Like a man testing his eyes I stared at her face. It was beautiful.

"What would you like to do?" I said, and saw on her lips, as I had the first time, the soft knowing smile of her tolerance. She took my hand and left on the flesh of the wrist the imprint of her teeth.

There were lights at sea, there was music on the waves, and there was love in the pollen-heavy air of Acapulco, but we coasted by gas stations that were closed, houses that were dark. We drifted down the grade to a traffic circle, one that I recognized from the map in my pocket, and we followed it around, the motor idling, to the left. In the lights ahead I saw the mound of dirt, the unlit lantern on the top of it, but I did not see the ditch from which the earth had been dug. Not until too late. I saw it as the wheels, both front wheels, dropped into it. The drop jarred the Greek out of my lap, killed the motor, shut off the lights, but left the radio playing a familiar version of "Perfidia." After a pause Mac said:

"Man, what's that noise?"

"Xavier Cugat," I replied.

"I mean *that* noise," he said. "You know what I mean," and I did. Behind the music I could hear the pounding of the surf, and one spinning front wheel.

"That's the wheel," I said, and it hardly seemed to matter, until the music stopped.

We hadn't thought to bring a flashlight along, so I

had to scratch matches to see what had happened. A ditch about a yard wide, and five feet deep, had been dug halfway across the road. The lantern on the bank of dirt had run out of oil. The car had dropped on its frame, leaving both wheels spinning, but one of the water lines had been broken. The water streamed into the ditch and smelled faintly of antifreeze.

"How's it look, man?" said Mac.

"Looks like we walk," I replied, and struck another match to see how he took that. He looked comfortable. Billie's pretty little head was on his shoulder. Her teeth were white.

"Why'nt we just stay here?" asked Mac. "Moon, water, girl, Chesterfields, what the hell?"

Rising up in the seat the Greek said, "Is that the sea right there?"

It was the sea. It didn't look more than forty or fifty yards from us. When the breakers rolled in we could see the foam piled up like sand.

"I'm going to take a dip," she said, got out of the car, unbuttoned the skirt of her touring outfit, kicked off her shoes, then walked away from us toward the sea. We lost sight of her just as she reached the beach. I had opened my mouth to say, "*Look*," but when she kicked off her shoes the word had stuck in my throat.

"She tight, man?" said Mac, since that explained whatever needed explaining.

"She'll be back," I said, and I had no more than said it and she was. She looked even bigger, with her body wet and shining, like one of those amazon channel swimmers, but the shorts and blouse she had worn down to the beach were dry.

"My God," she said, shaking herself like a dog, "go take one. It's wonderful."

Why didn't I? What I wanted to do was chase her back into the sea and run my hands over her body while it was cool and wet. What I said was:

"It better wait until morning. We've got to get to where we're going."

"Okay," she said, agreeably, and that cut me worse. She could take me or leave me, and I didn't want to be left. I ran up the windows of the car and said:

"We better take along at least a bag apiece. If we leave them in the car—"

"Ah'm—" Billie interrupted, getting out of the car, "Ah'm takin' all mah bags," and reached for two of them.

"Sure, honey," I said, "you and Mac."

"How far is it?" said Mac.

"It's not so far," I said, "if we happen to find it."

I picked a bag of my own, with what I'd need in the morning, two of the smaller cartons the Greek passed me, and Mac carried three bags, one drawn up under his arm, and Billie carried two. The Greek settled for some cartons and what she could fold over one arm. The rest we left in the car, under a lap robe, and I locked it up. In the morning the hubcaps would be gone but the boy who had swiped them would sell them back to us later.

"This way—" I said, leading off, and we crossed the road and went along another ditch. They were putting in pipes. Lengths of heavy black pipe fenced in the road. There were lights along the street, but the posts were so high they glowed on the sky like so many pale moons. It crossed my mind they were up there, out of reach, to keep the natives from swiping them. We walked two long blocks on the level, curving with the shore, then we stopped under a lamp to give Mac a rest. We had been walking on the level but we were all covered with sweat. Where Mac carried the bag under his arm his coat and sleeve were soaked. The pounding of the surf followed the curve of the shore, and went along over our heads like a plane's roar.

"Let's get goin'," said Mac, but we all just stood there,

listening. Between the blows of the surf we could hear
the thumping rhythm of the drums. There was no breeze,
it seemed to come from padded blows on the surface of
the bay, a pulsing beat that seemed to vibrate in the
heavy air. Without speaking to us, Mac picked his bags
up, started off. We went along behind him, single file,
to where the ditch itself turned and went up the grade.
I struck a match and read on the piece of curbing that
this was our street.

It went upgrade, very sharply, and on the rise where
it curved into the darkness we all stopped, panting like
dogs, and too winded to talk. Mac had soaked through
both his pants and his coat. When I struck a match to see
him he looked as wet as a slicker. All I could see of the
Greek was the white blouse she had slipped on over her
wet shoulders, but Billie, like the letters in a road sign,
had luminous points. Her big eyes glowed, and there
were large white buttons on her dark blouse. It made
me think of that dancer with her luminous breasts, her
bra full of crushed ice. In Acapulco, on a tropical night,
it seemed to make more sense. The body of the dancer
cool and sleek as a fish packed in ice.

I didn't see the man coming toward us in the darkness,
but I could hear the pad of his bare feet, and the ratchet-

like click of the gear of his bicycle. He swung wide of us to pass, calling out, *"Buenas noches!"*

"Buenas noches," I replied, striking another match, and saw the fish that he carried in a wire basket. They were still wet. The two or three on top were still alive. He wore a hat but no shirt, and one pants leg was rolled to just below the knee to keep out of the bike chain. His eyes widened just as my match went out. "The house of Señor Eroza," I asked, "it is near here?"

"Ahhhhh—" he said. "Señor Eroza!" making clear that that explained whatever needed explaining. He pointed up the road, on up and then above it, up the slope of the hillside above the tree line. I could make out a building with a veranda. It looked very nice.

"Señor Eroza?" I repeated, and he nodded. That was the *casa* of Señor Eroza. I thanked him, offered him a cigarette which he accepted, thanking me, then slipped it into the band of his hat and went ahead of us up the street. We followed him to where he stopped and waved us to go off to the left. A walk—a trail that soon would be a walk—went up the bank, between mounds of dirt, along a ditch that was fenced in with lengths of pipe. I thanked him again, and led off up the grade. After eight or ten steps I had to stop. The pounding in my throat made it hard for me to swallow, and I could hear Mac breathing like a swimmer gasping for air. My eyes burned with the sweat that ran into them.

We could leave the bags on the trail, I said, since we were now on the property, and after we'd had a shower, and a rest, Mac and I could come down for them. Nobody seemed to care. Even the Greek didn't answer me. Back in the road, where he had stopped to watch us, I could see the glow of the cigarette and the phosphorescent glow of one of the fish. In the street I hadn't noticed the smell. Now I did.

"Let's get goin'," wheezed Mac, and I led off again. Near the top of the grade there were steps in the slope, and a rail to lean on. The house was new; that is, under construction, since there were still mounds of dirt in the yard, bags of cement and sand, and several lengths of pipe. The house looked modern. That is, it called for glass. Glass was one of the things it called for that hadn't arrived. Chinese screens hung over the large openings in the walls. We stood in the yard, sour-smelling and shiny, and our breathing alone may have aroused Señor Eroza. In the opening where the door would be I saw him closing the front of his pants. He appeared to be a tall man for a Mexican. Tall and thin.

"Señor Eroza?" I inquired.

"At your service."

"We are friends of Señor Lockwood," I said.

He sucked the air between his teeth, threw up his hands, then turned to the door and called his wife. Then he stepped into the yard, grasped my hand, and said in a Spanish I found hard to follow that what was his was ours, although, alas, it was not very much. I thanked him, and he bowed to the girls. He repeated his greeting, this time to the effect that what was his was not much, not at the moment, but any day now—he let the wave of his hand take in the house and yard. The girls thanked him, and he turned to lead them into the house. A woman almost black, as tall as the Greek and twice as wide, stood there with a lamp and showed us the whites of her eyes. His wife. He asked her to show us the room. With the lamp she walked to the center of it, then placed the lamp, like a basket, on the top of her head. There she stood. The room flickering with shadows, in darkness herself. It contained a bed, one small child's chair, a fruit crate, and the front seat of a car. The walls were whitewashed. The floor was brick. A Virgin of Guadalupe was on the wall at the back. The flame of the lamp seemed to burn from the oil in the woman's head.

"There is no electric light?" I said.

Of course. That is, there would be. The wires and the poles were down there in the street. Perhaps we had seen them. Any day now they would be up. Any day now there would be lights in the rooms as well as on the porch.

"Ask him where's the shower?" said Mac.

"There is a shower?" I said.

Of course. An American shower. The finest apparatus to be had. It could be seen in the crate that was just to the left of the door. There would not be a finer shower in Mexico, once it was attached.

"There is water?" I was breathing less heavily. Almost calm.

"There is water," he replied, and raised a long thin arm to point at the ceiling, at the spot where he seemed to see it. Then he waved the finger, as one waves the traveler over a rise. The water was not there on the roof, nor on the slope of the hill, nor the hill beyond, but in a tank on top of the mountain. The biggest tank in the world. Any day now everybody in Acapulco would have more water than they knew what to do with, water to bathe in, to play in, wash their clothes and brush their teeth with, sprinkle the lawns and cool the streets with, even water to waste. There was water, and any day now it would flow right into the house. The pipes for bringing it down from the mountain were there in the street. The ditches for protecting the pipes from the thieves were there in the road. Had we not seen them?

I nodded.

"Well—" he said, smiled, spread his hands, and shrugged his shoulders. There was water. We would have it any day now.

"What's he say?" asked Mac.

"There'll be water any day now," I replied. My voice was not ironic. I was getting the feel of the place. Complaints are a matter for the authorities, and I sensed the absence of authorities. Any day now the water would appear. One waited for it. My eyes, growing accustomed to the light, could see the massive body of Señora Eroza, like a dark continent, beneath the dress she wore. He spoke to her, and with the lamp still on her head she left the room. She passed through the opening where the door would be, through the room where the shower would be, the light and water flowing, bountifully, once they were attached. We heard her speak with the accent of castanets, then the scuffling, hurried sound of frightened animals leaving a stable. No words. Just an exodus into the yard. Señor Eroza then beckoned to me and I followed him to the door of the room. His wife, a dark pillar with a flame, stood at the center of it. The room appeared to be about the same size, and with the same bed. But in one dark corner was an oil-burning stove, and on the wall above it a few pots and pans. In a fruit crate on the floor there were pottery plates, a bowl or two, knives and forks. Through an opening in the wall, where there would soon be a door, I could see the row of phantoms in the yard. All of them as God had made them. Two of them were boys. The boys still held on to the corner of the mattress they had dragged from the room.

"But Señor Eroza—" I began, and he closed his eyes, smiled. What was his was mine. Little as it was, that was how it was. In Acapulco one needed a roof—he waved a tired hand toward the lean-to in the yard—but not a house. And besides, any day now—

I thanked him. From the head of his wife he took the lamp, turned the wick up a notch, gave it to me. I turned to Mac, his sweat-soaked shirt and coat as transparent as an oilskin, his body like a large briny dill pickle in a plastic bag.

"Man—" he said, "how much dough we got?"

157

"Dough?" I inquired. But sometimes he will surprise you. He understood I was being ironic. "It's a lovely little villa," I said. "Which half of it you like?"

I did not smile. A simple statement of fact. Mac turned from me to look at his girl, and she looked cool. I mean she looked cold. Her hands were clasped in such a way that the fingers were curled up in the palms, the way they are in a game I used to play as a boy. The game went like this: Here's the church, here's the steeple, open the doors and there's the people. The fingers were the people. She was holding on to them. She suddenly crossed the room to the bed and put her hand on the mattress, as you would a radiator, then she came back to the door of the other room and said:

"In here."

I liked that. I had the feeling we were finally getting down to the facts.

"You can have the lamp," I said, passing it to her. "We like it dark."

She went off with the lamp, and that was how we had it. Dark. Through the hole in the wall it looked almost light in the yard. The Erozas were bedding down for the night. Was it something in the air? The pollen-scented night that fathered the thought? The Greek stepped out

of the room, she walked back to the door, where she
turned and kicked one shoe off, then the other, and I saw
the second one arch through the opening into the yard.
A new shoe. *Hecho en Mexico,* as the label said. Then
she slipped out of her clothes, tossing them on the bed the
way she did that night in Malibu, and when she had
finished she helped me take off mine. I got the coat off,
all right, but the sweat-soaked shirt had stuck to my
back. She took a grip on the tail and ripped it up the
center, like a sheet. That sound, like a sail tearing,
seemed to drown all the sounds of the night. For a
moment the pounding surf did not pound, the drums
ceased to beat. She had kept a grip on one half of the
shirt, and she used it to pull me over to the bed, and
before I could get my arm out of it I was tangled up with
her. Under the film of sweat on her body, the flesh was
cool. The bed had no springs, nothing to creak or twang,
but it also lacked one leg on the wall end, and the frame
had been propped on the wall for support. The knocking
sounded like someone trapped in the wall, wanting out.
It went on knocking, in fits and starts, since the Greek
has that sort of laugh, but there was no sound from the
family Eroza. Nor from Mac and his chick. When my
eyes were used to the dark I saw that the flicker on the

ceiling was lizards, almost flesh-colored, darting on the beams like pinpoints of light. There were also bugs, but no mosquitoes, a breeze soft as a bird's flight near the floor, and a night bird with the voice of a wailing infant in the yard. The pounding of the surf caused a tremor I could feel in the bed frame, where my hand touched it, and the Greek slept like a baby with my fingers in the curls at the scruff of her neck.

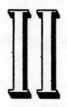

II

The two boys and a girl, the boys like sun-cured tobacco, the girl the shiny blue-black of a stovepipe elbow, stood at the foot of the bed staring at the white band left by my shorts. The body of a woman, one color all over, did not interest them. The body of a man, bleached white across the buttocks, did.

The Greek lay on her face, cupped in the hollow left in the bed by Señora Eroza, a large pear-shaped basin shaped by her hips. I lay on the plain, sloped like a beach, where Señor Eroza had left a few ridges. Knobs that he could cling to during a rough or wakeful night. Ridges that he could clutch when she heaved a sigh, or gently brushed him off. The sun, smoking like a blow-torch, rose from the sea where I thought it should set, and I sat up suddenly thinking we had slept both day and night. But it was morning. In the yard Señora Eroza sat braiding hair. Not her own, that had been done, but that of her oldest child, a tall, flowering savage with Rita Hayworth's mouth and eyes. The smell of urine and decay blended with that of the banana she soberly ate.

Out on the glassy bay, which I could see through the screen, there were pleasure craft, a large two-masted schooner, and the white streak where a surfboard, skidding like a coin, swung wide on a curve. On the slope below the porch there were flowering trees. On a branch near the door there were overripe papayas. The massive Señora Eroza sat like an idol before her own house.

As I would tell Mac, if he had the brains, or my Greek, if she cared to listen, Paradise, the one with long white shadows, was always the vision we turned away from, since there was nothing else, nothing human, that is, we could do with it. Nothing except hang it on the wall, like a painting, the way I would hang this scene in my mind. The Greek, a deep brown nude, and her white-buttocked lover sprawled on the bed. That picture I could grasp, but when I sat up in bed it broke like the mirror in which I saw it reflected. The little savages ran off, howling, as if the dead had come to life. They screamed the news at their mother, who ignored them, then they ran around the yard till they found their father and brought him back to the door to look at us. At me, that is. The dead man with the bleached buttocks who had come back to life.

Señor Eroza looked older to me in the daylight than he had at night. Older and thinner, his chin almost pointed, a sort of South Sea version of Don Quixote, his head spinning with the windmills that would pump water, any day now. He picked up his smallest child, the one hugging his legs, and while the boy chattered to him he ran a finger into his mouth, around the gums, and fished out something. Holding the child in his arms cost him an effort; he had to lean back and stand straddle-legged, but I was seldom to see him without one in his arms or two or more in his lap. Through a gap in his front teeth the tip of his tongue slipped in and out.

He greeted me, taking in at a glance my zebra stripe, the brown body on the bed, then matter-of-factly he predicted that a fine day lay ahead. With his five children he watched me rise, draw a pair of pants over my white spot, and with that matter settled they lost, as a unit, their curiosity. They turned from the room and looked for something to do in the yard. I slipped on a shirt, but left off my shoes because I liked the cool feel of the floor, the bricks moist as a shower room, almost soapy around the bed. In the white light I could see the dirt, the filth in the corners, the bugs in the mattress, and the bites I had scratched red and sore during the night. But I liked it better by day than by night. I liked the shimmering view of that dreamy bay through the bamboo screens. I let the Greek sleep, covering her legs with her skirt to keep off the flies, then walked to the door to see how Mac and Billie were getting on. I had to step across the room where the shower would be, once it was attached, and stand in the opening where the door would be, when the hinges arrived.

Billie Harcum was dressed, seated on the bed which she had partially covered with a beach towel, and I could see the spot where she had curved up like a kitten to sleep on it. She sat with her back to me reading about the fourteen frustrating "disturbers" that made the 44 Practical Ways to Happiness hard to come by. Mac—I had to look around for him—lay curled up on the car seat, his back to the wall, his head on a piece of her air-weight luggage softened by his pants. He had taken off his coat, but slept in his shirt, pants, and shoes. During the night he must have rolled off the seat, since about half of his shirt was covered with floor dirt. More dirt had stuck to one side of his face and one sweaty arm.

Love Among the Cannibals

There's a moment before rain becomes a snowflake, and a chick like Billie Harcum becomes Mrs. Macgregor, when you reasonably feel that it just might become something else. Or perhaps nothing in particular, just evaporate. But overnight, or in less than a night, you look up and see that the die is cast. The crystal has formed. You can't imagine it being anything else. Little Billie Harcum, of Ole Memphis, a piece of unfired Suthun pottery, had somehow passed through the flame and was now a piece of transparent porcelain. You wouldn't have to turn the saucer to see the potter's name on the back. Or where, like a tax-paid stamp, it would turn up next. Her taut little body—I suppose she tried to sit on the lip of the bed, without touching—was stiff inside the dress that had the price tag dangling from the belt. I don't like pity. But what else is there to feel? The way a bride, after a brutal honeymoon, will go through an album of wedding snapshots in order to recover the clichés she had just lost. On the bed at her side was a pamphlet entitled *Acapulco, Lovers' Paradise*, a souvenir album of post-card views she had picked up. Shots of the night clubs, the Copacabana, where the revelers danced barefoot in the sand to the cha-cha-cha and the American jazz from the Club Canibel. Views of

Pie de la Cuesta, where, lounging in hammocks, you watched the dark-skinned boys dive from the cliffs into the sea, then swim like dolphins into the sunset, their mouths full of coins. All of it in color. The way it would look, the way it would feel. The dazzling strand, the glassy sea, the glamourous nights of mambo, conga, and rumba, while her nonlover sprawled on the rumble seat, phenobarbitaled.

"Mornin', honeychile," I said, and it might have killed her. She drained white as her eyes. It took her some time to fight her way back from Norman Vincent Peale, and Healthier Living, to Irwin K. Macgregor and life among us cannibals.

"Yoh-all just get up?"

"Us-all didn't," I replied. "Just me."

She smiled in such a way that I knew she had managed to brush her teeth.

"Let me see what I can catch for the pot," I said, and stepped out on the porch, a sort of veranda, where Señor Eroza was coming toward me with a pail.

"Water!" he said, as if he had made it himself.

"To drink?" I asked. He made a face. It was the face of a man who had drunk and survived it. But he didn't recommend it. Not just yet.

"Any day now—" he said, pointing toward the mountain. Any day now the finest water in Acapulco. But not just yet. No, this water was to wash.

I thanked him. I took a cup of it and splashed it on my face. While I combed my hair he watched me, and I said:

"There are eggs? We would like to buy bread and eggs?"

Of course there were eggs. But later. Perhaps by noon. He, Señor Eroza, would see that there were eggs. But right now, no. Right now there was fruit.

I replied that we did not want to trouble him, but right at this moment we had no car. It might be a day or two. We had a car, a good one, but right at this point it did not work.

"A car?" he asked. I nodded. "Would it be red?"

I smiled agreement. Yes, this car was red. A bright one. I pointed down the slope to where we had left it. Near the traffic circle. His eyes lit up. Señor Eroza had seen it? I asked.

Did I think he was blind? Indeed, he had seen it. A fine car. He liked the color of red. It made him wonder, that color, what color the wheels would be?

"The wheels?" I replied. They had no color. They

were wire wheels and nickel plated. Hadn't he seen them?

That he hadn't, he said, since the wheels were not there. The body was there, and bright red, but not the wheels.

I stopped combing my hair and looked at him. He returned my gaze. I suddenly understood what he meant and said, "Ah, the hubcaps. So the hubcaps are gone?"

"Of course," he replied. Who would take the wheels and leave the hubcaps?

"They have taken the wheels?" I said.

In Acapulco wheels were hard to find. Good wheels with wire spokes were perhaps in demand.

I cupped a handful of water from the pail, splashed it on my face. Desperation makes me calm. Indeed, they were in demand, I said. Where would I go to buy them?

Nothing he had seen had astonished him. What I said did. He picked up the child that stood hugging his legs, then stepped back a pace to see me better. He smiled, shrugged, kissed the child, then said, "Who knows?"

I became even calmer. "There is a reward," I said, "to the man who will sell me the wheels."

That did not surprise him. I could see that he considered it sensible. "When I go for the eggs," he said, "I will mention there is a reward."

168

I thanked him.

He shrugged and said, *"De nada."* It is nothing. Another child ran to him and he put the first one down, picked up the second. He bounced the child on his arm and seemed to have forgotten what we had discussed. But he hadn't. "As for the top—" he began.

"The top?" I echoed.

A hole had been cut in the top. With such a top, it was a mistake to lock the doors. They had gone through the top to see why the doors were locked. It being none of his business he had not looked through the hole himself.

Still smiling, still holding the child, he turned from me to the house, bowed, and stopped smiling. I turned to see the Greek standing in the doorway, combing her hair. A celluloid dream of the tropics, she had slipped on her bra, her shorts, and put on the earrings with the green stones. She made quite an impression on us both, but on me it was favorable. Señor Eroza saw a woman who had failed to put on her clothes.

"Her clothes are wet," I said. "She went for a swim."

A false smile on his face, he turned to gaze at the yard.

"What are you saying?" said the Greek.

"That you are starving," I said. "That we would like to eat." I turned back to him and said, "There is fruit?"

Fruit, indeed, there was. It hung on the trees. He put down the child he held, spoke to her, and she ran off behind the house. A moment later she was back, with a papaya, and Señor Eroza placed it on a log block, the top pitted with feathers, and with a machete sliced it in half. He sliced the halves, then with his fingers scoured out the seeds, put a handful in his mouth. Through the crack between his teeth he spit them into the yard as he licked them clean. Papaya has a pungent odor. Some find it an acquired taste. The flesh is smooth as the lips of a woman and leaves a scent in your mouth. With the first bite of it, that is, I thought of the Greek. I gave her a slice, then carried two into the room where Mac stood at the wall with his electric razor. He had plugged the cord into the wall socket, but nothing had happened. He looked at me.

"No curnt?" he said.

"Any day now," I said, "direct and indirect, hot and cold, but not right at this moment. Right now just papaya."

I held out a piece.

"I don't like it," said Billie, and backed away.

"You'll learn to," I said, sucking up the juice. "Filtered water with a flavor to it."

I stood there eating mine like a piece of watermelon.

So did the Greek. She drew a brown hand across her wet mouth and wiped it on her new shorts.

"Greek," I said, matter-of-factly, "Señor Eroza has his Latin standards. A good woman should be heard but not seen. Not in shorts."

"Say I go without them?" she replied.

"That wouldn't bother him, but it would me."

"What does it mattah what *he* thinks?" Billie put in. "Weah not goin' to live heah—ah we?"

I went on eating papaya.

"Man—" said Mac, "we gotta have curnt. We gotta have a shower. We gotta have a piano. We got work to do, man. Ain't that right?"

"Last night you asked me a question," I said. "You said how much dough we got? The answer is not much."

"Man—" said Mac, retrenching, "we gotta have a piano."

"The best things in life are free," I said, looking at my Greek, "but curnt, showers, and pianos are luxuries. I mean they cost money, like some women. You know what I mean?"

He did. He looked at her and she said, "Ah didn't come down heah to live like a niggah. Ah can live like a niggah right in Memfus, wheah I was born."

"Look, honey—" said Mac, "they ain't really colored.

She's just one of these big, darky-lookin' gringoes."

"A niggah mammy brought me up," said Billie. "You-all can't tell me nothin' about niggahs."

"He probably wouldn't let us stay if he knew that," I said, and nodded my head toward Señor Eroza. "He probably thinks you're mostly white, like the rest of us."

She didn't hear that. She had suffered too much to suffer any more.

"The chick's hungry," said Mac, "she's gotta eat. She'll feel better when she eats."

I turned to the Greek and said, "You like it here?"

"I like it here," she replied. Her mouth and all one side of her face had the Valspar sheen of papaya juice. A melon. A ripe melon of a woman. One ready to be sliced. She even smelled like a melon, thanks to that papaya, and I watched the pleats form in Billie Harcum's upper lip. She had to curl her fingers up tight in her palms to get a grip on them.

"Baby—" said Mac, and put his hand out toward her, but when a spark jumped the gap he jerked it back. "She's gotta eat," he repeated, mechanically. "She'll feel better when she eats."

"We'll go down to the beach," I said, "then I'll get a cab and go after some food."

"A cab?" said Mac. "Ain't we got a car?"

"Right now we ain't." I said. "We won't have the use of the car for several days."

"Ah still have some things in the cah," said Billie.

"You mean, you did," I said.

"What you mean did?" said Mac.

"Past tense of *do*. Señor Eroza says that our type of car is very popular. The wheels, that is. For the moment the wheels are on loan."

"Look—" said Mac.

"We will when we go by," I said, and walked back into our room, sat on the bed, and put on my socks and shoes. The Greek came in and stood there while I was lacing them up.

"You mean that about the wheels?" she asked.

I nodded. "I also mean it," I said, standing up, "about the dough, that there isn't much of it, and about the fact that the best things in life, *my* life, are still free."

I said that knowing that she might not take it, but she did. She took it, then said:

"Do *you* like it here?"

I took a moment to think. "I'm afraid," I said, "I like it where you are. Curnt or no curnt, shower or no

173

shower, piano or no piano, dough or no dough."

I'm also afraid that she took it for granted. Like everything else. She licked the papaya juice from her fingers, then took off the shorts—for Señor Eroza—and put on, for both of us, the skirt of her touring togs.

"Do I need shoes?"

"You should always have something to kick off."

She put on some shoes, then we went out on the porch where Mac and Billie were standing, Billie with her beach bag, her gem-framed dark glasses, her sunsuit with the price tag, and her coolie-type beach hat. Mac wore his Hawaiian shorts, his lisle socks, and a straw hat he had bought from a kid at one of the stop-lights. All the Erozas were down at their end of the porch, and Señor Eroza had a child in his lap. When he saw the Greek in her blouse and skirt he stood up, holding the child, and gave her a bow.

"To the beach?" he inquired.

"To the beach," I replied, and we went down the slope, skidding on the gravel, edging along the ditch that would soon hold the pipe, and would then carry the water up to the shower, when it was attached. On the turn, where the street banked into the sun, the Greek had a trim of fire around her head and shoulders. When I looked back up the slope the trees seemed to smoke with heat. We went along single file, walking on our shadows, following the ditch at the side of the road, then we crossed it to where the mound of dirt blocked the street and looked at the car. All four wheels were gone. The rear end was still on the boxes they had used to hoist it up. The nose of the car was in the ditch as if trying to hide. We stood there beside it, shading our eyes, and the glare from the paint made it hard to look at it. I waited for someone to express how I felt, if I still felt anything.

Mac said, "What'll they do with just the wheels?"

"Sell them back to us," I answered.

The moment I said it I knew they wouldn't. They would keep the wheels and add the car to them. The idea was so crazy, once it crossed my mind, I knew it was right. I had brought along my car keys but I didn't need them to look inside. They had slit the convertible top open, neatly, and folded it back. The rear seat had been pulled forward so they could get into the back.

"What did we have in the back?" I said.

"The sound tape," said Mac. "All the tape and the records."

"We'll charge it to production," I said. He didn't reply. They had left one of the cushions, the bottles in the door bar, the radio in the dashboard, and the rearview mirror.

"Ah will nevah even know what ah lost," Billie Harcum said.

We cut across the empty lot where a signboard advertised that a new modern hotel would go up there, any day now. Information on request. Any day now work would begin. At the sea wall we stopped and looked at the beach. The tide was out. A stretch of trackless sand sloped to the sea. Banked against the sea wall was a tangle of driftwood left by the tide.

"Nobody here but us chickens," said Mac, but he was wrong. On wooden posts, down the beach to the south, were two birds so big I thought they must be turkeys, until the near one, catching my eye, flapped along the beach like something learning to fly, his long raw neck exposed to the light. No one else saw him. I didn't trouble to point him out. Out over the sea, cruising in tandem, a school of pelicans went by like a flight of bombers. One of their number, as if shot down, folded his wings and dived into the sea. He reappeared a second later, gulped his catch, and rose into the air.

"Make yourselves at home," I said, "while I go to town and get us something to eat."

"Need me?" said Mac.

"You stay with the chicks," I replied.

I watched them go down to where the sand was clean and a mist of spray blew off the water. Under the hair on his legs Mac was the color of the white sand. I watched the Greek drop her skirt, slip off her blouse, and then for my benefit turn and face me. A licking flame seemed to outline her body, smoke in her hair. I waved, then walked back across the empty lot to the street.

I walked a half-mile, maybe farther, before I found a cab. He had driven out from town to park where some palm trees shaded the street, and there was water, in a nearby fountain, for washing his car. An elderly man, he knew a word or two of English, and answered all my comments with a flat okay. I told him I wanted food, lots of it, with some thermos jugs to keep it hot and cold. He let me sit in the car until he had finished washing it, which took some time. Above his rearview mirror he had a little Virgin of Guadalupe, lit up with electric candles. Dangling from the mirror he had a miniature saddle and a pair of boots.

Since I had seen it last, Acapulco had grown, but looked and smelled the same along the water. Nor had it changed very much along the street he took me up. I bought a basket in one shop, two thermos jugs in another, and since the beach would fall under production I picked up a beach umbrella and four folding chairs. Then we rounded up the food. It was all prepared: it didn't take time to cook but it took time to buy. It took time, that is, to bargain for. When he saw I didn't seem to know the value of money my cabman took over, asked me to sit and watch his car while he took the money and went and bought what he thought was good for me. What he thought, that is, *we* could afford. Only the best was good enough for us—so you can see it took time. But by noon we had the grub rounded up. Two fat birds, whole; we had what they call *molé*; we had *tortillas* wrapped in swaddling bands, and I don't know how, but we also had two buckets of beer, on ice. Something he described as *gusanos de maguey* I later found out to be maguey worms. I mean I found out too late. Mac ate them like potato chips.

I let my cabbie fleece me for the fare as a further indication that I needed his protection, since it was plain— even to me—that I did. I mean, we all did. In a place like Acapulco a friend is a man who knows you are helpless and still likes you. He holds you up for a spell, then you hold him. He buys something from you, then you buy it back again. This flunky was my man Friday, he seemed to know how to live on the beach, and he helped me put up our new umbrella and the folding chairs. There was not a soul on the beach when we walked up. I had never before seen Mac *in* the water, but he had crawled into it to get out of the sun. He still had his hat on, his shirt on, and sat like a fat kid waist-deep in the surf, tossing rocks into a hole that Billie Harcum had scooped in the sand. Way out on the bay, maybe two hundred yards out, my Greek was floating like a rubber raft. When I yelled and waved the new umbrella she rolled over and swam in. The cabbie helped me pitch our camp on the beach, then he stood to one side, at a respectful distance, and waited to see what the rest of us looked like. I'm afraid we *looked* the same. I mean to say that we needed his help. I asked him to join us for a bite of lunch but he declined, first mentioning his family, then the fact that his work was so demanding that he had no time for such things. He moved back to the sea wall and sat on it watching us eat.

We ate all of one turkey, we ate all of the *molé*, and we drank all of the beer. Just watching us eat had made the cabbie drowsy, and he had dozed off in the shadow of the sea wall. After his siesta I asked him if he could find the time to get us some more beer, and if he happened to know where we could rent a portable radio. He said, "You leave to me." He said it in English, and in such a way that *leaving it to him* was not unusual. He had our number. And I was glad that we had his.

I left it to him, and came back to the umbrella where the heat, the food, and the beer had us all pretty sleepy. We all dozed off till the frothy lick of the tide woke us up. We moved our camp back along the sea wall, collected driftwood for a fire in the evening, and when it cooled off both the Greek and I went in for a swim. While we were out on the bay the cabbie showed up with more iced beer and a radio. He didn't stay to see what we would do with it, however, nor wait for me to come out of the water. From the sea wall he waved, his teeth white in his face, then he went off.

A little before sunset we ate the second bird, what was left of the *tortillas*, and finished off the beer. We saved the thermos of coffee for breakfast in the morning, and as the beach darkened we lit our fire. Not so much for the heat or the light, as the company. We dug warm pits in the sand and lay there listening to the radio. There was a fire to the south, perhaps half a mile or so, and in the light on the water we could see the bathers, maybe hundreds of them, in the surf before the big tourist hotels. But no one had come within earshot of where we were. It seemed hard to believe that life was really worth living anywhere else. Lights ringed the bay, in the dusk so pale they didn't give off light so much as collect it, holding it cupped like a match until it was needed after dark.

We had come down to the beach to get out of the house, to get away from the bugs, the lizards on the ceiling, and the smell of urine and decay in the yard. We had come to the beach, that is, to talk over *what next*? Whether we would blow what little dough we had for a villa, one with curnt, clean sheets, a shower, and a piano —not any day now, nor tomorrow, but *tonight*. We had come down to the beach to make some sort of decision, but there had been no talk. Didn't they care? Any more than I cared myself? In that villa on the slope we *had* cared—Miss Harcum had cared so much she could hardly stand it—but here on the strand, in the languorous air, we seemed to have found what we had come for. If we hadn't known what we had come for, at least we recognized it. We had come to strip down like so many white shadows in the South Seas. Portable pagan love songs drifted to us from across the bay. On the lids of my eyes, my private Cinerama, I could see that tanned lover, Ramon Novarro, singing to that first dream of love to be packaged in a sarong.

Had we come to the end of the perfect cliché? A love song with the languorous beat of the surf, a sea as warm and heady as a toddy, with the sun and the sand in the Kodachrome of heart's desire? Whether we had come for it or not, we had it: it seemed to be what we wanted, and when we left the beach it was only to go to bed.

The car, stripped of its chromy assurance, looked more real by night than by day; it didn't dissolve in a shimmer and we stood for a moment, silent, looking at it. During the day someone had made off with the radio. The chrome trim on the lights had been unscrewed, the bulbs and the reflectors removed, and the chrome handles had been taken from the doors. Mac had a look inside, and said, just in passing, that the seat they had left might be good to sleep on. So he carried the seat, and the Greek and I carried the folding chairs. We had learned about the grade and took our time going up the slope. Señor Eroza and his family were out on the porch, looking exactly as we had left them, except that a girl, rather than a boy, was now in his lap.

"A good day?" he asked.

"Wonderful," I replied.

Had I observed the car?

"It is not good," I said.

"Not without wheels," he said.

"Not without wheels, lights, and door handles," I replied. We smiled at each other with international understanding and good will. Then Señora Eroza, smoking a Delicado, stood in the center of the room, the lamp on her head, while Mac and I made a bed out of the two car seats. If she thought it a strange place for a man to sleep, she gave no sign. We set up a folding chair in such a manner that it would support his legs.

We let them have the radio, and the lamp, then walked through the door to our own apartment, where we undressed in the dark, lay down on the bed. The moon had not yet come over the mountain, but the sky was light. In the yard, under the lean-to shelter, the Eroza family gossiped like chickens, and then, as if at a signal, the gossip stopped. I could feel in the frame of the bed the pounding of the surf. The tide was still rising. It would smooth over our tracks and hiss in our fire. I let my hand touch the body of the Greek, glide along the film of sweat on her arm to her shoulder, from there to the scruff of hair on her neck, which I gripped.

"You know what day it is?" I said, since it had occurred to me that it must be the day on which I had met
her. I had known her for a week. For a week, that is, I
had not known her. "You know what day it is?" I repeated, and gave her head a shake, but the only sound
from her was a whinny. That sound she made when I
was about to kiss her, which I did.

I woke up about sunrise, scratching the fresh bites on my legs. I had rolled from the slope into the basin Señora Eroza had left in the mattress, since the Greek, who had filled part of it, was not in the bed.

In less time than it took me to scratch a bite, I was on my feet. Listening. Jumping up the way I did had startled a bird that had been in the room, and it flew around wildly, slapping the screens, until it found the door. The surf had stopped pounding. It now rolled in with the sound of a rug unrolled. I'm either looking for the crime that justifies my fears or punishment for the fears that are justified. I stood there listening. For what? The puppy-like whinny of the Greek making love. The rhythmic thump of a bed on the wall. Instead I heard music. Did it come from across the bay? At the door between the rooms I peered in to see the bodies sprawled on the bed, a sweaty tangle of limbs, but Billie was curled like a kitten, on her beach towel, and Mac lay in the hollow of the car seats, Between them, on the floor, the portable radio whispered of Latin love. But fitfully. Left on all night, the batteries had run down.

Then I thought of Eroza, the lean, Latin lover, but he slept like a child, his knees drawn up, in the shadow of the dark mound of his wife. Around her lay her farrow, top, side, and bottom, to make one mattress do. In the rubbish pit at the edge of the yard, like a Phoenix rising from the ashes, the raw head of a buzzard cocked one eye at me. But no Greek.

Almost running, I went through the door to the front porch and stumbled on her. She sat there leaning on a post, idly scratching her bites. Her hair was mussed, and one eyelid was swollen. Where had she found the chewing gum?

"What the devil!" I said.

She looked at my legs, at the bites down on her level.

"Soap—" she said, "soap stops the itching."

"Why the hell didn't you *say* something?" I said, and put my hand to my face. It was sweating.

"Say what?"

"Look—" I said, "I wake up out of sound sleep—"

186

She was smiling.

"You think that's funny?"

"Without their pants," she said, "I think men are."

I had been so upset I had rushed out there without my pants. Or anything else. I went back into the room and slipped them on, came out again. I sat down on the porch and helped myself to one of her cigarettes.

"Can I help it—?" she asked.

"Help what?"

"That you don't trust me?"

"I trust you," I said, "to do just as you like, and knowing what you like—" I inhaled deeply. I was too damn upset even to care how I felt. "All you had to do was touch me and say—well, hell, just say anything—"

"You were asleep."

"Was that why?"

"I wanted to sit here alone."

I made a face as if the sun had hit my eyes.

"Well, that's plain enough," I said. I made as if to get up, but when she didn't stop me I sat down again.

"I'm alone. You're alone. Why is it wrong to admit it?"

"It's not," I said, "but why rub it in?"

She didn't bother to reply to that, and I went on,

187

"Now I'm rubbing it in, I suppose, hoping to convince myself of something I don't really believe. I rub it in because it feels so good when I stop."

She ran her hand through my hair and said, "It's full of sand now. The way I like it."

"Just before I went to sleep I thought of something. Something I wanted to ask you."

"What?"

"If you knew what day it was."

"I don't." I let her think, and she said, "Well, what day is it?"

"I met you—we met—just a week ago."

I waited for her to say something. Anything. After some time she said, "I have to be so careful about your feelings."

I changed my position so I could gaze at her face. One eye was bite-swollen. Her lips and nose had been burned by the sun. As I have said before, she is not at all distinguished in the parts. I looked into her one eye, then at her mouth, for some clear sign of the lack of moral fiber, the softness and incipient decay of a girl of that type. Her one-eyed gaze held mine. Her lips filled me with nothing but desire.

"It occurred to me," I said, "that now I *haven't* known you for one whole week."

"What is there to know?"

I thought a moment, then said, "Do you miss your piano?"

The hand that rested in my hair took a firm grip on it, twisted my head around. She held it out before her, like the Gorgon head of Medusa, and I saw the pupil of her eye grow large. Then she released me, snapped her gum sharply, and said, "No." After a pause she said:

"What are you thinking?"

"That's the first time you've ever asked me," I said. She didn't deny it, or seem to care. "What am I thinking?" I said, and thought of something. "I don't *know* you—but I know you better."

That amused her. Smiling she asked, "What do you know?"

"That you like one piano better than another."

"Maybe so," she said, gripping my hair again, "but I play them all. They are all pianos."

"So all pianos are equal," I said, "but some pianos are more equal than others."

She took my head as if she meant to crack it like an apple. Then she let it drop.

"One wouldn't know that if one didn't play them all," she replied.

I had an answer to that, but I kept it. Good as an

answer is, you can't hug and kiss it. If pianos *unequal* to other pianos were not played—where would that leave me?

"This particular upright piano—" I said, drumming on my chest with my fingers, "is one that came in with the silent movies. It's not equal to much. But it's at your service, nevertheless."

The sun had given her the smell, almost flinty, that gave her skin its peculiar flavor, and I leaned forward, my chin on her knees, to take a bite of it. I crooned:

> "Baby, cannibelle, I fear its true,
> Something called my love is eating you—"

But before I managed I heard someone right behind me, humming the tune. Mac. He was there, both hands scratching, in the door.

"Scuse me for buttin' in, man," he said, his voice full of heart and husky, "but Christamighty, man, that was great. You get it down?"

I didn't reply.

"Gee-zus, man—" he said, cleared his throat and sang:

> "All pee-anos are equal, ta-ta-dee-dane,
> But this piano unequal to the strainnnn.

This li'l piano is your pee-annn-ooo
Neva-tha-lesssssss!"

The Greek was laughing. I raised my head from her
knees and turned to Mac.

"Christamighty, man!" he said. "What a theme. Every
li'l chick is her own piano, every li'l piano needs its own
tuner, every li'l tuner—"

"Is an old song-and-dance man," I said, but he didn't
hear me. The theme and variations had carried him
away. He stepped out on the porch just in time for the
sun to strike his face. He was bug-bitten, sunburned, and
from the way he dug at his crotch he was also lousy, but
he looked great. Every li'l piano had him transformed.
He had that smile on his face he usually reserved for the
Million-Dollar Baby at the jewelry counter. He also had
her. She was right there behind him in the door. He
turned to her and crooned:

"Every li'l chick is her own pee-an-oooo."

But when he reached for her keyboard it slipped away.
He wheeled back to me and said, "Man, I gotta play
somethin'!" and faced the yard, as if he might see it.
The Eroza kids, all five of them, were fanned out in the
yard waiting to see *what next*.

"There's your piano," I said, and pointed at the chop block, which sat about as high as a piano stool. I never thought he would, but Mac strolled over, dusted the feathers off the top, then sat down on it. Straddle-legged, he took a tuck in his invisible pants, placed his hands in the air, on the invisible keys, then lidded his eyes while he fingered for the lost chord. He found it, sounded it, then turned his lover's gaze on the Greek. Dreamily, he crooned:

> "This old piano, baby,
> Is down on its knees,
> The strings are missing
> And so are the keys,
> But I don't mean maybe
> This old piano, baby,
> Is yourrrrsssssssss.
>
> When we start kissin'
> There's no chord missin',
> I'm easy to please
> If you're the kitten on my keys
> Baaaaaa-beeeeeee."

Eyes lidded, lips parted, he went on softly fingering the invisible keys. One hand he placed in his lap, like Liberace, with the other he played his love song without words, while the Erozas, white-eyed with wonder, stood gazing at him. On the air—the faraway tinkle seemed to drip from his fingers, like drops of water—we could hear the fitful, fading whisper of the radio.

"How's that?" he whispered, leaving a note suspended.

"Sounds familiar," I said. "Would it be Gershwin?"

It would. He gave me that smile which expressed his pity for the cynical type.

"You gotta start with somethin', man," he said, and beamed a smile at the Greek, "so it might as well be good."

"We'll start you with a piano," I replied, "a real piano. It's more your type."

He didn't seem to care. He sat there happy with the one he had.

"Every li'l chick's her own pee-an-oooo," he crooned, and swung into "What Next?"

We had fruit and what was left of the coffee for breakfast, then we loaded up with beach chairs and headed for the beach. On the way we paused to see what was left of the car. It appeared to have crawled deeper into the hole, since both the windshield and the top were now gone. The hood had also been raised, and work on the engine had begun. The spark plugs, the carburetor, the oil and air filters, and the battery were gone. I examined the job from the professional standpoint. It was fairly clean.

"We gonna charge this to production?" Mac said, and it crossed my mind that we should. It was part of the production. What part? The purest part of a cannibal's love. I took a card from my billfold, leaned on the fender to make a few notes. Mac opened the umbrella to stand beneath it. In its hot green shade he stared at me, and waited. The girls had walked on ahead of us to get out of the heat. I let them move out of range, then I sang:

"A cannibelle's affection is the other way round,
　She builds you up by tearing you down.
　She strips your chassis,
　She drains your gas,
　She leaves you like an oil smear in the underpass."

"Man, I'll buy it," said Mac flatly, and put a hand into his pocket. He drew out a stick of gum, divided it in half, gave a piece to me. Under the beach umbrella we crossed the empty lot to where the women, standing on the sea wall, had turned to see what was keeping us.

They looked great. They looked extremely well fed, that is. A lovely pair of cannibelles, sunned and scented, waiting for the boys to bring up the pot, build the fire, then hop in and be stewed. Before we reached them, I heard this voice hallooing at us. My cab driver was there in the road with his cab. This time he wasn't alone. In the seat at his side were three or four kids. I hollered at him to wait, then I asked the girls if there was any little thing they wanted. The Greek wanted filter-tip cigarettes and chewing gum. Billie wanted soap. She also wanted paper, of the sort that came on a roll.

I left Mac in the shade of the umbrella, and the girls standing on the sea wall, and came back through the glare of heat to the cab. Since I was a special deal, he put the kids in the rear, let me ride in front. I said we'd want the usual thing, only even more of it, along with some batteries for the radio, some cigarettes, soap, and some chewing gum.

"Anything else?" he asked.

We exchanged glances. I wondered how he knew, then I said, "And a piano."

He turned the car in the road, headed it back toward town.

"A what?" he said.

"A piano," I repeated.

"On the beach?"

I shook my head, casually. "No, not on the beach. Right now we would like it where we live."

"And where was that?"

I told him. In passing I mentioned the name of Señor Eroza.

"Ahhhhhh—" he said, and looked at me with understanding.

"You know him?" I inquired.

He nodded. After a mile or so he added, "A fine place. Electric lights, shower, water, any day now."

"A piano, too—" I said, "any day now," and he agreed.

We bought chickens this time, roasted young fryers, fresh pineapple we had sliced and stored in a thermos, cans of the long green beans we could eat without cooking, some sweet rolls for breakfast, cigars for me, Kleenex for everybody, and a DDT bomb. To get some live batteries, however, we had to run down a fellow with a portable set, then persuade him to rent the set to us. That took time. On the way back I bought ice-cream cones for everybody in the car, and three more for the beach, which I gave to the kids to run ahead and deliver for us. Before we reached the sea wall with the load of food, one of the boys ran at me with a melting cone. What was the trouble?

"There were only two people," he replied.

I was holding the hamper. It held me upright to the spot. I did not need to ask which one was missing.

"She will be swimming," I said. "She likes to swim," then we all walked ahead to the sea wall where we could look. The tide was out. In the heat perhaps the sea was drying up. Mac stood deep in the shallow water, waving his arms. I could see nothing on the surface of the bay but an outrigger canoe, with a small patched sail, and beyond it a motor launch anchored a half-mile or so offshore. I dropped the hamper in the shade of the umbrella and ran down to Mac.

"What's up?" I said.

Without facing me he said, "She went in for a swim, you know what I mean? She went in for a swim, an' the next thing we knew—" He stopped there and waved his arm, a little wildly, at the bay. When he looked back at me I may have looked sick. He put his hand on my arm, said, "Man, don't get me wrong, you know what I mean?"

"NO!" I screamed. "What the hell *do* you mean?"

He turned and flung his arm toward the bay again, in the direction of the boat.

"Next thing we knew, man," he said, "she was on the damn boat. We saw them waving at her. Saw them pull her aboard."

I didn't reply.

"Man—" he said, "it was her. It took three of them to do it."

I think it would have been better, in Mac's opinion, if she had drowned. His idea about boats anchored that far offshore was the same as mine, and it wasn't a good one. Out there, on the deck or in the hold, life was led without its prohibitions. An anchored boat was worse. *All* the hands were free, that is.

I walked back to the wall and told Señor Carrillo, my cabman and sponsor, that everything was all right, everything was hunky-dory, since my girl had just swum out to see a few friends. She would very likely swim back to the beach in an hour or two. He saw I was lying and it made him unhappy. Even the kid with the ice-cream cone knew that I was lying. He let the cone melt. He didn't want to eat the ice cream of a lady who had drowned. I walked back to the umbrella where Billy had put out some of the food, and cut up slices of the chicken, but just the sight of food almost made me sick. I felt the same as I did the night I met the Greek, only worse. I knew what I wanted. I had the taste of it on my lips.

"Ah told him—" said Billie, wagging her little head, "ah *told* him to leave huh alone."

"You told him *what*?" I barked. I may have yelled it.

When I wheeled to look at Mac his jaw hung slack. He got it working again, said:

"Look, man—will you *look*?"

"I'm doing nothing else."

"Woman—" said Mac, turning on Billie, "Christamighty, woman!" and I watched this little chick peel off a slice of the chicken, the way you would a strip of sunburn, and drop it into her pretty mouth. She licked her lips. That piece of flesh had been peeled from the three of us. In just a soiled little handful of words she had had her revenge.

"Ah doan mean to say he *molestut* huh," she said, letting us think it over while she sucked on an olive, "but he ackshilly did egg huh on, Uhl, honey. He re-ah-ly did."

"Man—" said Mac, hoarsely, "you know what I did?

199

Just to make a li'l chitchat, you know what I did? I asked her if she happent to have a li'l girl friend somethin' like herself. You know what I mean? Just to kid her a bit. You know what I mean?"

"He wantut a li'l curl so much lak huh," said Billie, "he didn't want to take the trouple of waitin' foh huh."

Mac took off the straw hat he was wearing and sailed it down the beach. He ran his hand through his hair, and at a loss for words, for gestures, for song hits, he picked up a thermos, shook out a handful of the ice cubes, chewed two or three of them up. The water ran from his mouth and dripped on his dark linen beach shirt. If he had been in the Greek's line of development nothing on sea or land would have kept them apart. She hadn't swum out to sea to avoid it, she had swum out to sea looking for it. I knew that. He knew it. We all knew it.

Out on the bay this boat had swung around on its anchor while I stood there looking at it. The tide had turned. I could see people in the deck chairs, sunning themselves.

"All I got to say is—" said Mac, "she's gonna miss a damn fine lunch," and he took some of the olives, popped one into his mouth. All he ate was the one, the rest he tossed, one at a time, in the direction of the buzzard that had pitched his camp on the post nearest us. I missed that lunch too. Billie Harcum and the buzzard ate the white meat.

I couldn't sit there on the beach, staring at the boat, so I asked Señor Carrillo to take me into town. In town I would try to find out whose boat it was. That sounded sensible. It also gave me something to do. Mac followed me back to the cab as if he intended to go along.

"This chick crazy, man," he said, "you know what I mean?"

"She likes to bolt," I said. "We all like to, but she does it."

"Look—" said Mac, "you mean she'll bolt with anybody?"

"She bolted with me," I replied. "That answer your question?" It did and it didn't. "But if I were *you*," I added, "I wouldn't get my hopes too high."

"Man—" he said, "you gone and got yourself a call girl—"

"Right," I said, "a will-call girl. She will call it the way she sees it. And she just did."

He saw I was temporarily out of my mind.

"If she comes in while I'm gone," I said, "don't do anything Billie wouldn't do," then I got into the cab beside Señor Carrillo, and we drove off. As we curved along the shore I had a good view of the motor launch. It had turned so I could see that the flag it was flying was American.

"A good day for glasses!" said Señor Carrillo.

"Glasses?" I said, and thought he meant dark ones.

He took his hands from the steering wheel, cupped them to his eyes, made a focusing adjustment.

"Ahhhhhh—" I said understanding, and he exclaimed:

"Many powers!" as if wishing me health.

In my condition I needed a man like Señor Carrillo, one who knew before I spoke that I would be lying, and what I needed was a pair of strong glasses to increase my suffering. In love we all have the Latin temperament.

"Where does one buy them?" I asked, but to need them was not the same as to buy them. He saw again that I did not know the value of money, and needed protection from myself.

"The boat will come in soon," he said; "it will be nearer," meaning I would not have need of the glasses, and that my eyes, weak as they were, would be more than strong enough. He was right. The boat was on its way in by the time we had reached the wharf.

Watching that boat come in—watching the movements on the deck, the young men in sailor pants that hugged their firm bottoms, the young women in middy blouses and white sailor hats—I had time to dump the Greek overboard, out of my life, then haul her back on deck again. The error of her ways, the error of my ways, the central error of our ways together I could see very clearly—I could see that it didn't matter, that is.

The launch was named the *Sea Beast*, the deck was covered with frogmen flippers, diving equipment, and large glass jars full of sea life and ooze that they had dredged up. A floating marine laboratory of some sort; the crew looked like vacationing football material, with a sprinkling of chicks noted for their mental development. The girls wore cameras, held small nets, and were plainly what Mac called the brainy type. The young men were tanned Gods. But they were too young for my Greek. She was not on the deck, nor anywhere in sight until they had the boat tied up, and the plank down, when she came up from below wearing one of the sailor hats and a middy blouse. The way she looked in that outfit you can imagine, but I was glad to see more on her, rather than less, and trailing her up the ladder was this bug-shaped oldster in the walking shorts. He was loaded with what I would estimate to be several thousand dollars' worth of camera equipment, and he gazed up at me through the long-range half of his bifocals. A friendly, disarming, ladybug-shaped, ridiculous man. He wore a skipper's hat trimmed with fishing flies, a UCLA track shirt, and a lifetime of sitting, or squatting, had left his knees permanently cocked. He was holding a jar, in which something floated, a fish line with weights for sounding the depths, and I seemed to recognize, at a glance, the Greek's new line of development.

Three or four of the boys ran the gangplank to the pier, and the girls came up first, my Greek waving, then she took my hand to offer it to Dr. Leggett, who gripped it eagerly. He wanted to apologize, he said, for depriving me of Miss Baum. They had drawn her from the sea, like a mermaid, and she had assured them all that she would not be missed until they put in at the pier, which they did soon enough. It was just one of the strangest things in the world to be anchored in the bay of Acapulco, and draw out of the water, like a fish, one of the UCLA alumni. There was nothing affected or suspicious in Dr. Leggett's surprise. He was always turning up something unheard-of in the sea, and now he'd turned up this. I suppose she may have told him that I was her uncle, her guardian, or some such stooge, since she was Miss Baum and I was Mr. Horter right off the bat. He took us both by the arm and we went off to have a drink.

We sat on the veranda of that seedy hotel that faces the wharf, with the fine view of the bay, drank Sidral, bottled water, and learned about the sea-ooze sources of life. Dr. Leggett was a marine biologist. In the jar he held before us was some of the primeval ooze of life. It made him stutter to contemplate it, and when he stuttered the Greek supplied him with the word he wanted.

"Thank you, my child," he would say, and place his freckled, sunburned hand on her own. Platonic. Absolutely. But what was it that disturbed the primeval ooze, what was it that got it to oozing, that is, if it was not a pair of deep-sea hands meeting like that? One platonic, the other pulsing with the juices of life. When I peered into that jar on the table, green and fermenting, what I saw was myself. If my sap was drained into such a bottle, it would look like that. Behave like that. And if the Greek's hands were then cupped around it, it would ooze life.

Along with the Sidral I had a bowl of peanuts, I held a hundred or more colored slides to the light, and I listened to a lecture on my own lovesick condition, which I did not understand. All of it mystifying, marvelous, primeval, underwater life. All of it exactly as I knew it to be in myself. Leggett was somewhere in his fifties, his teeth were not good, his breath was bad, his knees were bony, but strange things can lie in the path of a girl's development. I had, for example. Nothing fished from the sea could be stranger than that.

Did he arouse her desire? It hardly mattered. Something in her was aroused. If it was not her *own* desire, it was for *his*—his passion for a bottle of sea-green ooze. So much—I couldn't help thinking—like the Greek herself. A solution of animal, vegetable, and mineral, in the process of becoming something else. Bolting, that is.

Nor was it lost on me that the professor's passion, however platonic in its intentions, had undergone a transformation in the magnetic field of the Greek. His passive ooze had picked up her charge, the percolating signal was being passed along the network, and one fine moment, placing his hand on hers, he would feel the spark. *My child*—he would say, and undergo a shattering development. The sea-green fermenting ooze would not be in his bottle, but in his blood.

When he finally ran out of slides, and bottle water, I managed to put in that our party, back on the beach

206

where we had left them, might be wondering about us. It brought him up a little short. It almost crossed his mind that all was not well. He had talked so much he had a froth on his lips like strips of meringue, which he kept licking off, and for one long moment he sat stiffly erect looking at the Greek. It was pitiful to see it. Here was a man who was known to have one losing his mind.

"My, my, my—my—"

"Child," she added, and he placed his freckled hand on her own, then gazed at the table covered with all of his gadgets and spring-wind toys. His bottle of ooze, his metal case of slides, the notebook of sketches he had made underwater, and an oyster with a pearl in the process of formation. He pressed the oyster on her. He had lost his mind, but he still thought he had one, saying in a loud voice, to indicate he meant it, that he had taken the liberty of asking Miss Baum to join the group. There was room. The cabin for girls had one more bunk. He could not, in justice, give her full credit for the course, but for one who had come from the sea, as she had—

"I'll have to think it over, Dr. Leggett," she replied, accepted the oyster, and got up from the table. When I stood up beside her she gave me her hand. One of the triumphs of my life was that moment; the other, of a similar nature, was when a cat who hated men had her kittens in my lap.

"Be seeing you, Doc," I said, feeling friendly toward him, knowing how he felt ever better than he did. He sat there, with his toys, and watched us walk across the street to the cab. Señor Carrillo, still waiting for me, was even more relieved than I was, and we took seats in the rear of his cab and he drove us off. She took my hand and said:

"Isn't he wonderful?"

So long as she was holding my hand I could admit it. I agreed, but I was also still human.

"You just happen to meet out in the bay?" I said.

"I looked up—" she said, looking up as if she saw him, "and there he was! He said, 'Good heavens, a Siren!' "

"A poet!" I said. "He should be a song writer." She released my hand, and I went on, "We like to kill the ones we love, I suppose, but in my time we didn't brag about it. I can see the times have changed. Any suggestions for burial?"

Why did I talk like that? We might as well have turned the car around, at that point, and driven her back to Dr. Leggett sitting there with his ooze, his stutter, and his colored slides. But we didn't, we drove on, along the streets where the palm shadows were crossing, and she suddenly said:

"I was wondering why you didn't."

"Didn't what?"

"Didn't kill me," she replied.

"My God," I said, "don't talk like that."

"When you love me," she said, "you know what I think? I think, if he would kill me now, I wouldn't care. I would love it."

I took her head in my hands and turned her face toward me. She had said what she meant. I looked at her eyes, her lips, and the knowledge that one day they would be gone made me so ill that I dropped my head in her lap. She took it between her hands, like a child who is sick, kissed it to help it recover, then wiped from my face the film of sweat. Señor Carrillo had pulled over to the curb and stopped. He got out of the car and said:

"I will go tell them you are here," and he hurried off, almost trotting, then he turned and called, "but there is no rush. I say there is no rush." I watched him hurry ahead, trailing his shadow, then go over the sea wall and drop out of sight. He did not reappear. I don't know what he told them, but nobody appeared.

"Come—" she said, and helped me out of the car, but

we did not cross the empty lot to the sea wall. We crossed the road and went along the ditch to what was left of the car. During the day they had taken off the bumpers and the engine hood. The radiator and the top of the block would be gone when I saw it next. Somehow, that idea pleased me. I took off the shoes and the shirt I was wearing and tossed them into the car, what was left of it, the way the Greek had stripped down and tossed her clothes on the foot of the bed. I could see she liked that, and since she was still wearing the silly sailor hat and the middy blouse, she tossed in the hat, then peeled off the blouse and threw it in. We got to laughing, the way you will when something is stirring you can't quite control, and I took off my pants and tossed them in, then the candy-striped shorts I was wearing, and she took off and threw into the seat her swimming shorts. Stripped down to the point where God had made us, such as we were, we walked up the slope. I held her hand—I mean I reached out and took it the way Adam would have held on to Eve—and then we went along the ditch where the water would flow, if and when the pipes were laid, and up the grade to the house where there would be light and power, any day now. We didn't pass anybody going up the grade, nor were the Eroza kids waiting for us in the yard, but Señora Eroza, dozing on the porch, rocked back her head to gaze in our direction, but what she saw seemed to be a natural part of the world of her dreams. In her dreams, that is, she too walked around holding hands. She smiled, not so much at what she saw as how pleased she was to see it, then her head rocked forward and when we walked past her she was asleep.

I remember we went in through the hole in the wall, but we both stopped at the door to our room. What was wrong? The Greek stood smiling down at her feet. They were the color of the sand in the yard, but that was not it. They were almost as big as mine, but that was not it. She had come to the door, this time, with nothing more to kick off.

Did that mean, I wondered, we were leaving the Garden—or entering it? I stood there, a troubled Adam, until my Eve took a grip on my hand, as if to reassure me, then she led me into the room.

IV

Leaving them alone like that was what did it. Alone on the beach. Leaving them with the sunset, the pounding surf, the cha-cha-cha, and the languid heat—there is nothing like heat, and the heat alone might have been enough. Why do we say that every bitch is in *it,* if it isn't the heat? On top of that you have to put the bewitching night, and the way the Greek would whinny when we made love. One might argue that *that* did it. But one would be wrong. They didn't do it in the hope of more of the same, but in the certainty it would be less for us. Some people can't bear to see other people have so much fun.

I was lying there pretty much as God made me, with a few minor alterations, when Billie Harcum came to our door and peered in. Radiant. All brides are radiant.

"Mac an' me have an announcement," she said. She

said *have a nounsemunt* the way you have a baby, a mortgage, a divorce.

When I tried to reply the sound stuck in my throat. I would say her real triumph came at that point. Behind her pretty radiant little mask I could see her eyes flare up with a gemlike flame when she saw the effect on me.

"Mac an' me ah gonna hitch ah wagon to a stah an' get married," she said.

You can't improve on that, and I didn't try to. I just lay there till the bed began to tap on the wall, and I knew that the Greek, sprawled on her face, was laughing. I sat up and put my feet on the floor to steady the bed.

"What a great day this is!" I said, loud enough for Mac to hear it. "I can hardly wait to congratulate the lucky man."

The lucky man did not reply, and Billie said, "Ah nevuh seen a grown man look so relaxt. Ah'm wonderin' if the preachuh's gonna have to come heah to marry us."

I thought he might, but not because Mac was so relaxed. I dug around in my bag for a pair of shorts, then followed Billie to the door of their room. Irwin K. Macgregor lay out on the bed, a beach towel around his waist. The word for it was *bushed*, not relaxed. He had made his way from the car seats, and the beach chair, to the chambered heart of the boudoir. He had won the laurel, that is, but lost the fight. I had often told my colleague Macgregor that of all the men in the world he had the most to win, since he had the least to lose. But I was wrong. He had just lost something important to him. His Million-Dollar Baby was now his dime-store wife.

I had come in to ridicule him, but I just stood there. He smiled like he was sick.

"You feel all right, Mac?" I asked.

"Man—" he said, hoarsely, "I feel great."

"We both wan a simple suhvus," Billie said; "we wan a simple civil suhvus," and the way Mac looked it would be a funeral service. From his back, he rolled over on his face. He was like a kid coming down with something, fearing the worst.

"A simple civil suhvus," Billie repeated. "All I wanna do is get it ovuh with."

"I know," I said, and she saw that I did. She didn't care. She could play her cards in the open now. She had been up for some time since all of her clothes, from the three bags she had salvaged, were spread out on the car seats, the beach chairs, or hooked to the wall screens.

"Uhl, honey—" she said, "foh a reahly simple suhvus, what you suppose I should weah?"

214

We had the happy bridal breakfast on the veranda, featuring sweet rolls and coffee, and since we had plenty of both I asked the Erozas to share it with us. The kids had rolls but no coffee. Señor Eroza described it as an expensive taste. Sensible children, like his own, would not acquire it. He went on to say—stimulated by the coffee—that although circumstance found him in Acapulco, his heart and soul were still in Yucatan. Hadn't I remarked the difference in his speech? I replied that I had. I may have also observed, being an observant man, that the true Yucatecan, a man like himself, had little in common besides the language with the Mexicans. Yucatecans were clean, thrifty, slow to anger, quick to right a wrong, generous and proud, with something of the blood of the old Mayans still in their veins. Mexicans were— excepting Señora Eroza, who was more of the Maya than of Mexico—Mexicans were like children. His own excepted, that is. In his home in Yucatan the lanterns would be lit, the ditches would be dug, the pipes would be laid, and the toilets would flush with a roar that would almost be frightening. If we went to Mérida we would see that for ourselves. The streets clean, the women lovely, the men cultured, the children quiet, the skies always sunny, but the sun giving much less heat.

215

While Señor Eroza talked he crouched like an Indian, his chin between his knees. With his long hooked beak he resembled a bird, one of the buzzards with his crown balding, shifting his weight from claw to claw as he perched on his post. The coffee widened his eyes and set his tongue to wagging—but put his wife to sleep. Señora Eroza, a cigarette between her lips, her great bust strewn with ceremonial ashes, sat upright with the smallest of her brood wide-eyed in her lap. He had the Yucatecan nose, and would keep it clean, but his eyes came from the islands and would lead to trouble. While we sat there a car honked in our street, and Señor Carrillo, leaning out to wave, asked if by the purest chance we might be in need of his services? I replied that we were, and he lit a cigar while waiting for us.

Marriage? A *civil* marriage? It took Señor Carrillo a moment to think. That was no marriage at all, of course, but one of the kind that were made north of the border. But what was made north of the border was also made in Acapulco. Made and unmade, that is. He was relieved when I explained that this thing was not for me, but for my friend, who looked sick. Mac sat between the girls, in the rear, his face sallow in the shadow of his helmet, like a missionary stuffed and dressed for the pot.

I leaned out for a look at our car as we drove by. The radiator and the block to the engine were now gone. Anything else? The man working on it dozed in the front seat. Having worked all night, I suppose, he had earned his sleep. On his feet were the shoes I had tossed into the car, and on his back was my shirt.

We had to make several stops. The documents could be purchased, for a consideration, but they had to be signed. An English clergyman, retired, with a panoramic view of Oxford in his study, conducted a civil suhvus admirable in its simplicity. Very brief. I'm a little vague on the details. When I have a guilty feeling my eyes avoid any sort of focus, like a shoplifter. A small dog chewed the laces of my shoes during the ceremony. I remember the bride's puckered lips—I mean, I remember her kiss. At the front of this house, supplied with a camera I had no idea Mrs. Macgregor possessed, I took a snapshot of the bridal party. Testimony. I remember focusing on the serene face of the Greek. Too serene. One tap of the chisel and the marble smile would crack. Señor Carrillo, his hat off, peered sharply slantwise at Señor Macgregor, with the eyes of a man who is paid to keep what he knows to himself. Billie Harcum Macgregor, the ring on her finger, held the license clasped

like a high-school diploma, her radiant smile beamed
in the direction of Mac. He gazed directly at me. Not
at the camera. It was one of those cameras you look down
into; you focus what you see on a ground glass, so that
I seemed to be—in Mac's gaze—in two places at once.
In the cool eye of the camera, and the one that he sought
in the top of my head. The appeal men make to the
assassin they had assumed to be their friend—an *et tu,
Brute* appeal—was on Mac's face. It gave me the creeps.
I couldn't take my eyes from what I saw on the glass.

"Will you *snap* it?" said the Greek, and I snapped it.
I have never seen the print. When I think of the wedding,
it's the ground-glass picture I see. What I saw there
altered my feelings—the way an assassin's might be
altered—after he has pulled the trigger, and he sees
what he has done. Had I got my man? No, he had
escaped. The man I had shot was some sort of nameless
stand-in for him. The man I wanted—Irwin K. Macgregor, first-class slob and second-class song writer—
slipped out of focus when I pulled the trigger, when the
shutter snapped. In his place, in his pitiful shoes, I had
caught Adam Macgregor, most pitifully nude, with his
ever-fair Eve green and swollen with the apple she had
picked, but did not eat. Stand-ins, perhaps, but not people, figures in a frieze symbolizing the eternal bride, the

eternal groom, and the eternal deception they played on
one another—being true to one another in order to be
false to everything else.

"Uhl, honey—" Billie said, when I looked up, "Uhl,
honey, yoh fohgot to wind the shuttuh!"

Did I? I wound it again, said aloud, "Hold it," and
focused on them, the Greek serene, the clergyman smiling, Señor Carrillo leering like a bandit, and the happy
bridal pair, petrified with affection, about to kiss.

"There," I said.

"Is it all ovuh?" asked Billie.

"All ovuh but the shouting," I replied, and said,
"Hooray!"

"Hoo-ray," Mac said.

In keeping with the simple service, we had a simple
lunch. Under the ceiling fans of an open-air drugstore
we ate hamburgers, American style, while Señor Carrillo
rounded up the makings of the bridal feast. We could
have blown what little dough we had and gone to one
of the clubs or big tourist restaurants, but one of the
things we seemed to have lost was a taste for that sort
of thing. It had been stripped off like the chrome on
the car. A bride and groom call for something special,
however, this bride and groom in particular, and I told

Señor Carrillo to let himself go, not thinking he would. But he did. He came back with a freshly roasted suckling pig. This little fellow had green gumdrop eyes, a soiled ribbon around his neck, and an American flag *hecho en Mexico* where his tail should be. As we drove south along the bay, with our pig, I could see Dr. Leggett's *Sea Beast* at anchor, the flag flying, the frogmen equipment scattered on the deck. Was he anchored out there waiting for the Greek to make up her mind? I could see a rope ladder, as if for her convenience, dangling at the side. I could also see, in the rearview mirror, the too-serene Greek at my side, the drilled iris of her eyes at a pinpoint in the shimmering light.

That stretch of beach with its buzzards was habit-forming. We couldn't keep away from it. We pitched our bridal camp back near the sea wall, and watched the fleet of touring fishermen come in. Big-fish hunters from small places, loaded up with creels, reels, gaffs, rods, and head nets, perched like targets in the cockpit turret seats at the rear. Sometimes a gray-haired matron, a visor shadow on her face, sat there winding up her line like a run in her stocking, her husband barking signals at her through a megaphone. On the deck would be the swordfish, waiting to be weighed in and photographed.

We had begun with two buzzards, both of them a

little shy, but having tasted our food and sized up our situation the word had gone around, and we now had a small flock. They were patient birds, and sat along the sea wall like sentries. Now and then Señor Carrillo, shouting Spanish oaths, would seize a piece of driftwood and run at them, but I preferred them on the wall at my back rather than circling over my head. They did too. When he came back and sat down they would return to the wall.

About sundown we all went in for a dip and watched them gather, like crows on a highway, and pick over the bones and scraps we had left. At that hour the breeze died, and in the slanting light they cast shadows on the beach like monsters. A faint whiff of their odor, like decay, hung around our camp. A motor launch that might have been Dr. Leggett's, with lights in the cabins, cruised out about dark, the motor coughing wetly like a man with a cold in his chest. We had planned to stay and build a driftwood fire, toast the marshmallows we had bought, and lie on the beach listening to the portable radio. But we didn't. We gave them to Señor Carrillo, for his kids. We stayed until the tide began to roll in, then we started back.

A lantern with a steady flame marked the spot where our car had dropped into the ditch. It was held by a woman while the two men with her went about their work. One had crawled into the ditch, where he worked beneath the motor, and the other had crawled into the opening at the top. Both greeted us when we passed:

"Buenas noches!"

"Buenas noches," I replied. "How goes the work?"

"It goes well," one replied.

"But the night is dark," replied the other.

"But the night," I replied, "is the best time to work."

They agreed. I wished them good night, and the woman, lifting the lantern, said, "Go with God."

The piano I had rented, and forgotten about, was there in the yard when we came up. Also Señor Eroza. He had not known in which apartment we had wanted it put. To put it in the wrong one, heavy as it was, might be worse than leaving it out in the yard. So they had left it. In the light from the sky we could see the yellow keys.

Mac dropped the beach chairs like a man suddenly summoned, stepped up and sounded a chord. What chord? "What next?" naturally. After a week of inarticulate talk, he could verbalize. I had forgotten about a stool, but that chopping block of wood, pitted with feathers, raised him to where he could rock forward, lovingly, over the keys.

222

I asked Señor Eroza if he would mind if Señor Macgregor, a song writer, got in a little practice before he
went to bed. Señor Eroza did not mind. Quite the con-
trary. Did I not know the Yucatecans were born musical?
He left us there and went to get his Yucatecan family
out of bed. He returned with the lamp, which he set on
the piano, the Eroza kids formed a circle in the yard,
but Mrs. Irwin K. Macgregor, nee Harcum, not only
knew "What Next?"—she had done it. Without waiting
for her cue, she joined her man at the piano. She leaned
on it. The light from the lamp glowed on her hair, her
teeth were like pearls. There was no moon, that would
come later, but we had the bay below us, ringed with
lights, the sky like a shell above us, and the faint beat
of the drums. Music is like the weather. It depends on
how you feel. Seated at the piano Mac felt better, his
chick looked better, I *was* better, the Erozas were en-
chanted, and the Greek put her hand in my sandy hair.
Mac found the keys that would work, most of them, and
in her big, talky voice little Billie sang:

> "What next?
> The life of love I knew
> No longer loves
> The things I do.
> What next?"

"Ahhhhhhhhhh—" exclaimed Señor Eroza, "she has lost him!"

I knew that she had, but I said, "Not lost—just losing."

"Ahhhhhhhhh," sighed Señor Eroza, and made a clucking in his throat.

"Man," said Mac, "get a load of this—" and he sounded a chord. A new one—almost new, that is—and he stretched it, gleaming, like taffy. "What next, man?" he said, and I guess we are a great team, since I knew. I had my cue, and I also had the scene laid out for me. The tropic night and the sea, the piano in the yard, the ring of white-eyed little savages, like cannibal-*knaben*, and from the palm-strewn wings the pagan love song of us cannibals. "What *next*, man?" crooned Mac.

Smiling at him, I said, "They eat each other."

"Man—you crazy?"

"Take a tip, son—" I said, then I hopped up and sang:

> "Take a tip, *mon vieux*, from the lady spider,
> She has her lover deep inside her,
> When he asked her *what next?* Why she
> Dined on him most carnally."

"Carnally?" said Mac. "They won't buy it."

"They will," I put in, "once they try it."

I did a heel-and-toe number, à la Fred Astaire, then tipped my hat and cane in the Ted Lewis manner, sang:

"A cannibelle's affection is a dangerous thing.
She prefers the knuckle to the wedding ring.
The banquet of love
Is the one she cooks
Without the aid of how-to-do-it books."

"Man, I'll buy it!" croaked Mac. "What next?"

"What next?" I echoed, and wheeled to look at Mrs. Macgregor, the Million-Dollar Baby *aus* ole Memphis, and Mr. Macgregor, her piece of Christmas jewelry already turning green.

"What next, man?" yelled Mac, the way a gobbler would turn, with his head on the block, and taunt his executioner. He knew, God knows. What he wanted me to do, while he still felt good, was chop it off.

"That's up to you—" I replied, "and your baby cannibelle." Then I crossed the yard to where mine was sitting, took her hand and said, "Us cannibals are going for a dip," and off we went.

"Look, man!" Mac yelled, and came down on the keys with both his elbows. The ear-splitting racket made us run like kids from a haunted house. We skidded down the slope, and in the street below we just kept running, on down the grade to the highway, then along the ditch to where the woman raised the lantern to watch us pass. We stumbled across the empty lot to the sea wall, then over the wall to the beach, where we sprawled on the narrow strip of sand the tide had left for us. We lay there, winded and laughing, till the sea began to lick at our feet. Then we sat on the sea wall, our feet dangling, and watched a big two-masted schooner glide into the harbor like a phantom, her power cut off. We could see, against the sky, the lacy web of her rigging, and two spidery men out on her bowsprit.

"What a dream of a boat," I said, since she looked like a dream in the dusky harbor.

"A dream?" she replied. "What dream?"

"The dream of everyone on shore," I replied. We watched her anchor. In the quiet we could hear the slide and rattle of the chain.

"Am I a dreamer?" she said, in a way that made it clear she thought the idea pretty corny. She fancied herself a nondreamy realist.

"You're all dream," I said. "There's not even a line down your middle where you begin and the dream stops.

You live your dream, which is to say you're a realist. Living with you has made me something of a realist myself. An essentialist, that is. The little inessentials have been stripped off."

She didn't reply to that, and I went on, "I didn't know when I bolted with you that it was not to sleep with you in a warmer climate, but to love you in a language we could both understand. Earl Horter, the master of the cliché, did not say to you what he thought he was feeling, since he hardly knew, without the clichés, what it was he felt. If he talked about love in the language he knew, he cheated himself. He had to learn about loving and talking from scratch, and he saw that the first thing the lover destroyed was the mind in his body, since it had nothing to do with his body of clichés. The body was cannibal, the clichés were vegetable. Love among the vegetarians, that is, was verbal—it was made with participles, unmade with verbs, honored, cherished, and disobeyed with nouns. But love among the cannibals is flesh feeding on flesh. I've been living on your lips, the strings of your eyes, and you've been living on my heart, my lungs, and my liver. Essentials. The fatty inessentials cut away. If and when you get around to the hollow of my skull, I'll serve it up. If anybody asks us if these bones live—" I put out my hand and gripped a near one—"we can say yes, thanks to the essentials, thanks to the essential business of love. Such is the love song, Greek, of Earl Horter to his cannibelle."

Was it my feelings that kept her silent—or her own? She had to be so careful, as she had said, to keep from hurting me. But I would have her answer later, in her own language, one that we had fashioned between us, and I would settle for it until something better came along.

We sat there till the tide lapped on the wall and wet our feet. Out on the bay the dream boat dissolved into darkness, the mast lights blinked. Later, the moon arose, and on our way back we could see our car, with its nose in the ditch. The woman had gone. The men were still beneath, working on it. In the flickering lamplight I could see their sweaty faces, the whites of their eyes. A few more pieces, perhaps another night's work, and the car would be stripped down to the same point we were. What point was that? The one we were at. My cannibelle took a grip on my hand, and I crooned:

> "You've stripped my chassis,
> You've drained my gas,
> You've brought me, baby,
> To a new impasse.

Love Among the Cannibals

> A cannibelle's love,
> Of which I sing,
> Is a one-time rather than
> A two-time thing."

Walking up the grade I thought I heard a piano tinkling. That was probably just my imagination, but when I awoke, several hours later, the moon had moved over to shine on the yard, and the moonlight glowed on the ivory piano keys. I would have sworn I saw them move, and heard the first bars of "What next?"

V

But it was not imaginary music that woke me up. It was real, real Cole Porter, lightly fingered in the Macgregor manner, blowing loud then soft as it came to me on the off-shore breeze. The tune? "Love for Sale." Quite a little number for the morning after, but no connection. No intentional connection. It had merely crossed the groom's loving mind that there might be something there that he could swipe. What made a song good was being able to recognize it, as Mac liked to say.

It made me think of old times, old times in the army, when Mac would spin the seat of the piano stool, dust it with his knuckles, then sit down and improvise. I couldn't see him, but I could almost hear him, when he worked out something good, pausing long enough to leer toward me and say:

"You like that, eh?"

Well, I did, I still did, and got myself out of bed to say so, but the Irwin K. Macgregor who now sat at the piano was not the same man. He had shaved. The sunburned flesh of his neck was badly cut up. Strips of the bride's roll paper had been used to staunch his wounds. He had also put on his new Italian-style loafers, the imported pants of nubby raw silk, the shirt with full flowing sleeves, and on his head, level as a stopper, his green beret. To keep his new shirt collar clean a handkerchief had been tucked between the collar and his neck. He was a great one to sweat. Mrs. Macgregor had taken notice of it.

She sat at his side, her knees drawn up so that the heels of her pumps were on the edge of the chair, wife and pupil, listening to the Maestro improvise. She wore one of her simple peasant-type gowns, a full skirt lapping over the sides of the chair, her arms bare to the vaccination scar she loved to pick. A *simple* silver ornament gathered her hair, and a *simple* silver log chain encircled her throat. She also listened. Listening is now done with the lips and the eyes.

"Like that, eh?" said Mac. Not to Horter, of Macgregor & Horter, but to Mrs. Macgregor. She liked it so much that words failed her.

"Da-da-dee-dee-dee-da-da," she said.

"Mornin', Irwin," I said, knowing how it killed him, but it didn't disturb Mrs. Macgregor. She turned her big, soft eyes on me, and I saw very clearly that I needed her help. That I was about to get it, that is.

"Uhl, honey—" she said, "yoh-all leavin' us ah-lone was the sweetust thing yoh evuh did. We had the longest talk. Din't we, Hon? An' the moh we talked, moh we could see we both felt the same way. Now that we foun each other, all we wanna do is wuk. As mah honey-bun put it, what we all come down heah foh, was to wuk. So we both decided to tun a new leaf, which was jus what we did this mohnin'. Din't we, Hon?"

"We turnt sumpin', all right," Mac replied.

"Missus Macgregor—" I began, and watched Mac's head drop about an inch between his shoulders. He was squatted on the chopping block, head bowed, and I remembered that scene on the ground glass of the camera. I had shot him once. I didn't have the heart to shoot him again.

"One li'l thing we decided," she went on, "is that the beach is no place to wuk. It saps a puson's strength an I doan know what-all. We plan to wuk heah in the mohnin' an' maybe take a li'l dip in the aftahnoon."

"Why not a li'l air-cooled apahtmunt," I said, "where you two can wuk fah into the night?"

"Doan think we din't discuss it, Uhl, honey, but we both feel the atmospheah out heah is so impotun. We both pahticulah feel you do so well in this heah atmospheah."

That's how she sounded. It was more important than what she said. I mean how it sounded out there in that yard—how it sounded to me, to Mac, and in particular how it sounded to the Greek, in the room at my back. Something in the stillness of the air behind me—as if the Greek had stopped breathing—warned me that she was awake. That every drop of this Southern oil fell on the fire.

"We've been doing very well, thank you," I said, loud enough for the Greek to hear me, "but I think we might do even better if we were left alone."

Billie smiled her pleated smile. One of the decisions she had made that long first night was to hear no, see no, speak no evil.

"Mac took the most pahticulah trouble," she went on, "to say how impotun he considuhs yoh wuk, and what a pity it would be if anything whatsoevah—"

Right at that point Mac, sitting there as if drugged,

suddenly banged both hands down on the keyboard, making a racket that made the skin at the back of my neck feel tight. Then he stopped, as suddenly as he started, cocked his head to one side as if listening, and he heard—we all heard, I mean—the tapping on the wall. But it was no laughing matter. My police dog had rolled over to scratch a bite.

"—what a pity it would be," Billie repeated, as if she hadn't noticed the interruption, "if anything whatsoevuh should come between yoh, me, an Mac."

"Wonder what it would be?" I said. "Any guesses?"

"Yoh men!" she cried. "Yoh can be so chilelike."

"Christamighty!" Mac bellowed, hopping up from the log. "Whatta you say we eat? If I hear any more talk—" He took a grip on his beret and yanked it down over his ears.

"What about something new in a song hit," I said, and took my seat at the piano, pecked around for my tune. I found it, beamed my voice at Billie:

> "When you find the cannibelle of heart's desire,
>   Put your little homemade pot on the fire,
>   Plunk your chick
>   Into the pot,
>   Then jump in yourself when the water's hot."

"Christ, man——" said Mac, and took my place at the piano, ran off a few bars, then gave me my cue.

"The sweetest fat, not to mention the bones,
You'll no longer find in the temperate zones,
But in Acapulco
By the sea
Where I ate my cannibelle and she ate me."

"It's great, man!" barked Mac. "But will they buy it?"

"Noel Cowt might do it in Las Fegus," Billie said.

"Las Vegas, hell," I said, "they'll eat it up in Acapulco——" and turned to look at the Greek, in her shorts and bra, standing in the door. One eye was swollen shut. There was nothing particularly serene about her, she stood there with one hand in her hair, scratching, making a frying sound like a firecracker about to go off. She looked like hell. I mean she looked full of it. If she had gone off right then, and not later, we'd all have been a little damaged, but it might have been better than one of us being blown apart. Mac hopped up like it might be him, and yelled:

"Hey man, here's your gringo!"

Mac likes people, but he almost loves them when he

can slap a label on them like gringo. I walked to where I could see Señor Carrillo, his head stuck out of his cab, waving. He had his kids in the car.

"Honey bun," said Billie, to her man, "whyn't you go along with Uhl an' help him. Whyn't you go along so he can get back quickuh, an' we can all get to wuk."

That was the best offer he'd had since we'd arrived. "Let's go, man!" he barked, and ran off like a kid. I had to step inside to put on some clothes, and the Greek came to the door to watch me. There was something on her mind, but I wanted her to keep it there.

"Cigarettes?" I said. "Chewing gum, chick poison?" She didn't smile.

"If you happen to get hungry," I said, "there's a li'l Suthun fried chicken in the yard."

I smiled, but the Greek didn't. Very coolly, deliberately, she squeezed blood from a fresh bite, licked it off. I gave her swollen eye a kiss, as I passed, and at the edge of the yard I turned to look at her. She was smiling. I could almost see the feathers of the canary she had swallowed on her lips.

I walked down to the car where Mac was seated in the rear, and Señor Carrillo had his kids up front. They all rode with their backs to the windshield, their eyes on us. When we got to the highway I noticed that the car was stripped like something you might find on the beach. The little fish had eaten all the flesh off it. Out on the shimmering bay I could see the schooner, the dream boat that had come in at night, and I asked Señor Carrillo if he knew its name. He did.

"The *Dolphin*," he said, then he added, "She is on the way back."

"Back where?" I inquired.

"To the States. She is from California," he said.

I settled back in the seat, and Mac suddenly said:

"Man, don't you get that li'l girl wrong."

I didn't want to talk about her, but I said, "Which one?"

"Man, didn't you hear me say li'l?"

That should have warned me. He refers to all females as li'l chicks. When he doesn't, somebody else has sorted them out.

"I don't think I do get her wrong," I replied.

"She's the best friend we ever had," said Mac. "That li'l girl's got me an' your interest at heart."

"That's nice," I said. "That's certainly nice."

"You're darn tootin' it's nice," he replied, showing how much she had already done for him.

"She wash your mouth out with soap and water?" I said.

"What you mean?"

"Darn tootin' is a pretty strong term," I said.

"Now look here, man," he said.

I put my hand on his shoulder. We once had a little rhubarb of a serious sort, in which I proved to be a little quicker than he was.

"If you don't want to hear what I've got to say," I said, "sit there in the corner and don't ask me questions."

"Man—" he barked, "this is all for the team. This for our own good."

"Any changes in the line-up since yesterday?"

"There three of us now, man. This li'l girl's great. She about chewed my ear off talkin' about you. She thinks you're Cole Porter, Liberace, Noel Cowert all rolled into one. She thinks you're great. Thing that worries her is she thinks you got an awful bad break."

"I do too," I said, "but what the hell, somebody has to write the music."

"Just kills her to see you wastin' your talents with this chick you got. Thing that worries her is, the team. She says this chick's fulla designs. Bein' a woman herself, she knows how this chick's mind works."

"How does it work?" I said. I couldn't keep my mouth shut.

"She's got an ulterior motif—" said Mac. "If she didn't, you think she'd be doin' what she's doin'?" He leaned back to let me get the full weight of it.

"It just never crossed my mind," I replied.

"Way she sees it," said Mac, "she's got her mind set on a big fat part. Built the way she is. When the time for the showdown comes, why then she'll apply the screws."

"I don't feel any pain," I said.

"You crazy, man? You got a big reputashun. You're nationly known figure down here—with this chick. What the hell, man. You must be crazy with the heat."

We had moved around the bay to where I had a better view of the big boat. Two men were up in the rigging. I saw a rope loop out, then fall to the deck.

"If she wasn't that sorta chick," went on Mac, "you'd never get away with what you're doin'. Fact you do, proves it. Like Billie says. If she felt about you way Billie does about me, she'd have put her foot down just the way Billie did. Why you suppose, when we went an' got married, she didn't speak up?" I didn't reply, and he said, "Man, it's time you woke up. It's time you knew what sorta girl this chick is—"

"I do," I replied.

"You do?"

"She's precisely the girl I want."

"You—" said Mac, rocking back, "you want a—"

"Cat got your tongue?" I said. "Or is it just soap and water?"

"You know what I mean, man!"

"You bet," I said. "You probably mean whore or slut. Slut is probably the word in your mind, but with your clean little Lifebuoy mouth you wouldn't think of mentioning it. Besides whore, there's moll, which is a word I like, and it may be that a moll like the Greek is my dream girl, but the word I like best is just plain cannibelle. It covers the ground. My cannibelle and I seem to feed on each other, but I'd say that you and your cannibelle—"

Mac turned from me as if he heard a voice call him, stuck his head out of the car. When he kept it there, Señor Carrillo slowed the car down and drew over to the curb. We parked there at the curbing, in the sun, while Mac groaned and puked into the street.

"He is ill?" Señor Carrillo inquired.

"It is nothing," I replied. "Just something he has eaten."

To eat something, in Acapulco, and not keep it down

is not news. Passers-by walked in an arc around us, but did not slow down. We sat there, in a drone of flies, until Mac heaved back and slumped down in the seat. Señor Carrillo drove on and when we stopped at our beer joint I went in. I took more time than usual, bought more beer, but when I came back to the car Mac was gone. Señor Carrillo made the face of a man who was sick where he couldn't throw up.

It took us about an hour, I would say, to round up the food. When we drove back along the bay I noticed that my dream boat was on its way out. One sail was up in the rigging. The crew were busy on the deck. We drove along slower than usual just to keep our eyes on the bay. With the sail up in the rigging she cast a dark shadow on her own swell.

My man Friday helped me carry the food up to the house. One of the Eroza kids was out in the yard sinking beer caps in the dirt, like mosaics, and Señora Eroza, propped upright on her broad base, appeared to be asleep. You never saw a scene so peaceful. Was that what made me scared?

"Come and get it!" I yelled, just to break the quiet, but nobody did. I knew they wouldn't. Somehow I knew they *couldn't*. Not both of them. I stood there the way you do after you've felt a concussion in the air and are waiting for the noise, then I walked to the hole in our wall and peered in. The bed was empty. My police dog was nowhere in sight. Her shoes were on the floor, her touring togs were on the wall, but I knew that she had snapped the leash—I knew she had bolted *something*. I crossed the room to the hole in that wall, peered in.

Mrs. Irwin K. Macgregor was there on the bed. She was tied down to it. Her arms, stretched taut over her head, were tied at the wrists to the bed legs; her legs were spread and the ankles fastened to the legs at the foot. Both her legs and arms were tied down with rags, a gag of rags was in her mouth, but otherwise she was stripped like the car we had left in the ditch. Her simple gown had been torn up to make the rags with which she was tied. My police dog had not bolted her alive, nor even fed on the softer parts, but after sniffing at the flesh had kicked up a little dirt to bury it. The contents of the night pot had been rubbed in like an ointment, soaked into the bed.

"Billie!" I said, and put my hand to her face, but she made no sound. Her eyes were wide, too wide, and when I leaned directly above her they rolled, without meaning

242

or focus, past my face. There was a bruise on one side of her body but too big for a blow: where the Greek must have leaned while tying and anointing her. The occasional smear of blood was not her own. It would rub clean from her skin, showing no scratch. Her powdered face had been slapped until it was puffy, so that she looked as if she might have been crying, but otherwise she was all in one piece; there were very few marks. She had merely been crucified in her own rags, and cunningly stripped. A very cool, professional job. Not done in haste.

I cut the rags, took the gag from her mouth, and wiped off her face. I didn't have much hope, nor feel much pity, nor care much what I felt. In the general stripping down something had also been stripped from me. Pity for the inessentials, the soiled Rose of Memphis being one.

I sat there on the bed and Señor Carrillo, as if to shade us from the light, stood in the door. Without any warning, this kid began to sob. All in a whoop. A pitiful flood, then she let out this moan like an animal, and rolled over on her face. When I touched her she curled up like something that had shriveled from the heat. Wrapped up in those strips of rag, with loose ends at her wrists and ankles, she looked like a galley slave thrown to celluloid lions. Like most of them, however, since the script called for it, she would survive.

I left her there, and in the yard asked Señora Eroza if she had seen the other girl, the big one, and she replied that she had, waving her hand toward the street. I asked Señor Carrillo to stay with the girl, then went down the slope, almost running, since something stronger than a suspicion had crossed my mind. I was still running when I passed the car, where the night workers dozed in the seat, then I ran across the empty lot to the sea wall, where the sun was in my eyes. On the clean sweep of sand left by the tide, there were tracks that went into the sea, but did not come out. Out on the bay there was nothing. Nothing, that is, but the big dream boat. Our dream boat, out near the middle of the harbor, under motor power but her sails unfurling, and where the boom swept the deck I could see her. She was that big. Like a madman I waved my arms, I screamed like a bird. When I saw her arm wave I leaped from the wall and ran down into the sea. Knee-deep in the water my stampeding fear slowly ran down. The arms that waved by themselves fell at my side, my panic buzzed like a muffled alarm, and I heard someone splashing up behind me in the surf.

Señor Carrillo, his pants rolled to his thighs, stood knee-deep in the water prepared to save me. The cloud of anxiety in his dark face was even greater than my own. He seemed to think I was mad enough to try to swim it, or drown myself. We stood there together, washed by the tide, gazing down the bay to the open sea, joined in a fellowship of helplessness. We watched the last of my dream boat's sails go up, and puff out with the wind. When I came out of the water he trailed along with me, back up the tracks we had made coming down, back to the sea wall where we stood side by side, facing the bay. We stood there till the sails were out of sight. Then he followed me across the empty lot to his car, the door on the driver's side still open, and I waited while he unrolled his pants and put on his shoes and socks.

We drove back to town. It was his idea, not mine. We drove back to that hotel facing the bay where a little pimp in English walking shorts sold me, as he said, something he thought would interest me. This was not the *muchacha* he had along with him, but a post-card view with the following information:

Amerigringo in mans Rm.
Hotel Paloma

I didn't check on the *muchacha,* said to be *muy fino,*
but in the men's room of the Hotel Paloma, in one of the
stalls, we found our Amerigringo as described. In time
of trouble, my colleague Macgregor achieves one triumph of mind over matter. He joins that brotherhood of
man who seek out a dark, quiet, private place. This one
was very dark, there being no lights, and he sat on the
stool, his fists pressed to his eyes, an empty bottle of gin
on the floor at his side. Several *muchachas de Guadalajara* had apparently fleeced him—the pockets of his coat
and pants were turned inside out—as if they had all had
a try at him as he came down the stairs. Mac didn't
really like gin, but straight gin was the symbol of that
fine mad age he had never really lived in but had heard
a lot about, and he admired the sort of man that only
gin destroyed. The blurb on Mac's last Immortal Jazz
Album would read—it would, that is, if I wrote it—
something like this:

> Irwin "Mac" Macgregor, wizard of the keyboard,
> creator of the tunes on a million lips, was found
> in the john of the Hotel Paloma, in Acapulco.
> The hand of death beckoned to him at the height
> of his career. With his old friend and colleague
> Earl Horter, he was engaged, at the time of his
> death, in writing those immortal songs that will be

sung while men have hearts. Old Dan Cupid—so important in his life—this time shot an arrow that proved fatal, *una muchacha de Acapulco*, as they say, being too much for him.

He was not yet dead, merely stinking drunk, but he had managed to increase our production costs by one pimp, one quart of Gordon's gin, forty-five bucks in cash, one self-winding wrist watch, one Dunhill gold lighter, and one crucifix on a silver chain. One soiled Amerigringo was all his little *muchacha* had left.

We carried him to the car, like a sack, but even that little haul left me so winded I knew we'd never get him, without some help, up the slope to the house. On our way back, as we passed the car, I saw that the men had stopped their siesta, and I asked Señor Carrillo if he would ask them to give us a hand. They were glad to. Even without the usual consideration. It had become known that the car on which they worked belonged to me and the sick Amerigringo, and to help carry him to wherever he belonged was a very small thing. In exchange for an American car, so to speak, a Mexican lift. So they gave us a lift, the four of us, with a limb apiece, managing pretty well, and we placed him on my bed since the one next door was still occupied. Señor Carrillo, without my suggesting, made us both a small lunch.

On one bed we had a woman, half mad, on the other a gringo, completely drunk, far out at sea we had a castaway, and in the ditch what was left of our car. Stripped down. What was there left of us to strip?

Señor Carrillo took a certain pride in me, but not much. He stayed, that is. He fed me what he thought I should eat. After eating we smoked, and the new Mrs. Macgregor, trailing her rags like a mad Ophelia, came to the rim of the porch and looked at us. She was hungry.

"Pull up a chair—" I said, and offered her the chopping block.

She ate olives, drank her coffee without sugar, and black. I was struck by the beauty of her eyes now that she had looked at something through them. I also noticed the animal redness of her lips. It crossed my mind that she was a true cannibelle at last. There was blood under her nails, and on her lips was the sun-tanned flesh of the Greek.

Need I tell you who passed the hours in the beach chair that night? I set it up in the yard where I could gaze at the sea and the moon. I could not see beyond the bay, where the dream boat sailed northward, but I knew that its deck would be milky with the same moon. Never mind what else. I had undergone a sea change myself.

The thought of the Greek—the thought of her, that is, rather than what she might be doing—did not torment me. I thought of her all night. Just the thought of her, in my condition, seemed to be enough. I saw her brown arms, laced with the long nail scratches; I saw the strong wrist where she had been bitten—she showed it to me, that is, with that serene smile on her lips. She held, as was her custom, my amorous gaze. No words of love, no slogans of endearment, no promises or vows passed between us—nothing but the flow of my desire, and in return, the flow of hers. I did not burn in the hell of who, under that moon, might share it now. I blessed his luck. I took a certain pride in my own. Stripped down, like that car in its ditch, to what we referred to as the essentials, I possessed nothing under that moon but my past. That much I could take with me, if I cared to, and I did.

I got up at one point, took my seat on the chopping block, and poked around on the keyboard till I found my tune. I put the last touch to our comedy of terrors in this vein:

> "Love among us cannibals is short and sweet,
> There's nothing to a loved one that we won't eat,
> The smile we love
> Is the one we'll miss
> On the baby cannibelle that we just kissed."

Mrs. Macgregor, a tattered phantom in her rags, came to her door. In the green moonlight she looked as insubstantial as desire. From the room behind her, like her ghostly lover, a voice croaked out:

"Man, it's great!"

I gave a nod in its direction, sang:

> "In Acapulco
> By the sea,
> The little inessentials
> Are essentially
> Your heart and your liver,
> The strings of your eyes,
> The big as well as
> The little white lies,
> On the beach of love
> You strip down to
> The essentially
> Inessential you."

"Man, I'll buy it!" barked Mac. He meant that it was full of heart. I've never trusted his judgment, before or since, but that once he was right.

VI

What next?

Well, the hinges arrived for the doors, but before the doors arrived for the hinges Mr. and Mrs. Macgregor, on Mrs. Macgregor's suggestion, chartered a small plane for a flight to the States where they would get a needed rest from their strenuous work on "Love Among the Cannibals." Mac wired ahead for a ringside table at the Mambo, where they had not only found each other, but Miss Billie Harcum, of Memphis, had also found What Next?

On our way to the airport I happened to notice that the car was no longer in the ditch. They had put it back on wheels and pushed it down the road to where Señor Carrillo liked to wash his cab: there were palms along the street and they could work around the clock, in the cool shade. The men working beneath it were putting back the motor, the men working in it were putting back the dashboard, and the men not working were thinking of putting back the top. But they were sticking to the essentials. The little inessentials they were leaving off.

Why was that? I turned to ask Señor Carrillo.

Well—he replied—for one thing, if they put them back on, some no-good Mexican would only steal them; and for another, weren't they *in*essential? To the car, that is?

I could see that they were, but when we drew alongside I could also see that something was missing. Something essential. I could see that it was their car now, rather than mine. Essential to them, but inessential to me, now, were the keys. Señor Carrillo slowed the car to a stop while I tossed them in.

I was thinking of that when Mrs. Irwin K. Macgregor, her big beautiful eyes now drilled with real pupils, offered me her new, almost real, but still pleated lips. I thought of it when Mac gripped my hand and said:

"It's been real, man! You know what I mean?"

I not only knew what he meant, I knew he was right.

Stripped of all my inessentials I could plainly see the futility of it, the lack of principle of it, the essential anguish and hopelessness of it, and then I got to thinking, the way you will, of other things. I got to thinking of her lips, her eyes, and the street where she still lived. Any day now she might be back there with those damn kids. Any day now, with one on her hip, and that serene marble smile on her lips, she would come across the yard toward whoever it was, helpless, hopeless, and mindless as he was, but essential to what she called her development. I thought of all that, and I knew that, any day now, it would be me.